Witch Hunt

Chris Priestley

Hodder
Children's
Books

a division of Hodder Headline Limited

Published in Great Britain in 2003
by Hodder Children's Books

10 9 8 7 6 5 4 3 2 1

A catalogue record for this book is available from the
British Library.

ISBN: 0 340 86056 1

Printed by Bookmarque Ltd, Croydon, Surrey

Hodder Children's Books
a division of Hodder Headline Limited
338 Euston Road
London NW1 3BH

Contents

Dedication

For my brother, Dave.

Author's note

All dialogue and passages in quotation marks in *Witch Hunt* use the actual words of the witnesses of the Salem Witch Trials. The spelling and punctuation have been modernised and all italics are the author's.

Chapter 1

One Winter's Night Long Ago

Let's take a walk. It's night-time. It's cold – bitterly cold. Our breath rises up in front of our faces like smoke. Snow blankets the ground, frozen, twinkling; crunching under foot. The trunks of distant trees glow dimly by the light of our lantern, but beyond them there is a deep and inky blackness.

The night crouches over us, held at bay only by our tiny light, ever ready to rush in and overwhelm us should the flame flicker and go out. A chill breeze plays among the winter trees, making the bare twigs twitch and whisper.

Something shrieks in the distance. An owl? You hope it's an owl. You're sure it's an owl.

But you speed up anyway, and your hand begins to shake with something other than the cold.

There is a group of houses up ahead, one in particular just visible in the darkness by the stars it blocks out. The shutters are closed against the cold and the night, and a faint glow rises from the chimney; a trail of blue wood-smoke coils and flutters.

Light seeps out from a crack between the shutters. If we stand on tiptoes and press our faces against the wood, we can just see through the tiny, grimy glass windows into the room beyond. A fire crackles in the hearth and a small, blackened cauldron hangs above the flames. By the warm glow we can see a group of girls giggling and whispering. They are up to something.

They have a glass of water and an egg. One of them taps the egg on the glass's rim until the shell breaks and she lets the contents flow down into the water. They are playing a game of fortune-telling.

The trick is to watch the egg as it shifts and billows in the water and look and to try and find some kind of form in its coils that will give a clue as to the occupation of their future husbands; the kind of *tinker, tailor, soldier, sailor* game that girls have played for centuries.

The girls are giddy with nervous excitement and the thrill of the danger. The egg swirls weirdly, backlit by the candle. It does seem almost to be moving, as if somehow alive. The girls stare wide-eyed, half wishing that they had not begun. But the thing is done, and cannot be undone.

The swirling matter seems to find a form inside the glass; it seems somehow to take shape in front of their startled eyes. But what shape? What is it? What can it be? The candle flame splutters in the melting wax as one of them whispers what it is and the others recoil at the recognition. A coffin, that's what it is. It looks just like a coffin.

It is daylight now, and though it is still icy cold, the fears and jitters of the night are fading. Looking around we can see a scattering of houses and farmsteads. The girls we watched last night are already at their chores. We are in the hard winter of 1692 and this is Salem Village. Massachusetts. New England. America.

This is still the New World – to the settlers at least. These people are not quite Americans yet. Many of the older residents were born in England and it was as recently as 1620 that the Pilgrim Fathers landed in the *Mayflower* and founded the Plymouth Colony not too far south of here.

In fact the wooden houses with their horizontal planking – clapboards they call them here – are just like the ones they left behind in England. We could be in the county of Essex, England, rather than Essex County, Massachusetts – if it wasn't for the acres of space and the wildwood beyond; and of course, those *other* people living in this land.

The Native Americans – the Indians, as the settlers call them – have been pulled into vicious fighting between England and France, and their colonists here in America, allying themselves with one or other of the countries involved. Settlements are attacked and women and children carried off into captivity to be ransomed – "redeemed" – at a later date. Salem Village has not been hit yet, but it lives under a constant threat. It has a strongly built watch-house manned by local men to guard against attack.

The strange thing is that many of the captives, when given the chance to be returned to their villages, opt instead to stay with these "heathens", these "savages". Despite being stolen from their families and having often seen parents, children, brothers or sisters horribly murdered, they choose to stay with their captors. Why?

One of the reasons is that life in a village like this one is not a lot of fun. Life is hard and short for most people in the 17th century, Native Americans included, but these people's lives are made even harder by the strict discipline required by their particular Christian beliefs. These people are Puritans.

They call each other Goodman and Goodwife here, and they really *do* believe themselves to be extra-specially good. They believe they have been chosen by God; that they are the "elect", that they are "saints". But that does not make them complacent.

Puritans are on a constant state of high alert. And it is not just the threat of Indian attacks. Indians, diseases, storms – all the troubles of the colony – they are all, the Puritans believe, just tools of the *real* enemy... Satan – the devil.

The devil is everywhere, just waiting for his chance to pounce. And anything that might make a Puritan drop his or her guard is eyed with suspicion: high spirits, drunkenness, vanity, idleness. Puritans are not joyless but they are rarely joyful. They do not even celebrate Christmas.

The Puritans think that their way of life is so righteous that Satan must feel he simply *has* to destroy it. Satan is not just a symbol of evil to these people. He is as real as the sea or the trees. And so are his disciples; so are *witches*.

A witch, or so it is believed, is someone who does harm to others (or their property, crops or livestock) by magical means; by spells or charms, an evil look, wax images or dolls or simply curses. The settlers believe witches can bring sickness and even death. They are hated and feared.

The hardline Puritans who are fighting to keep control of Massachusetts also believe that a witch is a kind of secret agent for Satan. Someone who has entered into a contract with the devil; someone who has sold their soul to the devil and is working to bring down the Christian colony of Massachusetts.

Puritans work hard. Their only day off is Sunday, but then they have to go to church. In fact *everyone* has to – it is the law, Puritan or not. The service takes place in a plain wooden building called a meetinghouse, which is a kind of cross between a community centre and a church. The Puritans do not think you need a fancy building for a church. In fact they are dead set against the whole idea of fanciness.

The good people of Salem Village arrive at the meetinghouse in their Sunday best; men in tall black hats, if they can afford them, thigh-length coats, knee-length breeches, and stout shoes or boots; women in crisp white linen bonnets, full length dresses and hooded cloaks to guard against the cold.

In England, those who can afford it follow the latest French fashions for huge curling wigs – for men that is – and expensive clothes made of the finest materials, decorated with intricate embroidery and trimmed with silk ribbons and lace.

This kind of worldliness and vanity is viewed with great suspicion by the Puritans of Massachusetts. Here, clothes are plainer by far, with white lace just about the only decoration. Colours are usually drab and dark and, instead of wearing wigs, men tend to grow their hair long, parted in the centre and pulled back from their clean-shaven faces.

Church services are long – three hours in the morning and two in the afternoon – but there is an attendant on hand to poke you with a stick if you fidget or nod off. Men are separated from the women. The best seats in the house are at the front and reserved for the wealthy and influential.

Children are lumped in with servants in an upstairs gallery. They dress like miniature versions of their parents and are expected to join in chores from a very early age. Although boys are given some chance to let off a little steam, going hunting or fishing maybe, the life of a Puritan girl is very, very dull indeed.

And maybe that goes someway to explaining the fortune-telling incident. What a thrill it must be for those girls to go against their Puritanical upbringing. What better way for these bored village girls to wind up their God-fearing parents than to play at magic?

And if that parent just happens to be the village minister, then all the better. That's right. The house we peeped into is the parsonage, the home of the Reverend Samuel Parris. One of the girls we saw is his nine-year-old daughter, Elizabeth – everyone calls her Betty – and another his eleven-year-old niece, Abigail Williams, who lives in the house with the Parris family and their married slaves, John Indian and Tituba. Things are about to get a lot worse for Parris – and for everyone else.

Chapter 2

Betty and Abigail

Soon the whole village is talking about Abigail Williams and little Betty Parris. Their behaviour has become very odd. It is said that the girls are "getting into holes, and creeping under chairs and stools" and "uttering foolish ridiculous speeches, which neither they themselves nor any other could make sense of." Nosy neighbours start dropping by to see for themselves.

At first, the girls' bizarre activities are seen as a medical problem. Doctors are called in to examine the children, but say they can do nothing for them. Then one of these doctors – Dr Griggs from the village – says what many in the village have no doubt already been thinking all along: that the girls are "under an evil hand."

Then the whispering begins. Witchcraft. *Witchcraft*. The girls are bewitched. These settlers know all about fits like these, and their links to the devil, to witchcraft. They have seen all this before. Or rather, they have read about it.

In October 1684, the famous Boston minister, Increase Mather, published *An Essay for the Recording of Illustrious Providences* detailing the strange case of Elizabeth Knapp, who had fits so violent that six men were hardly able to hold her. She spoke in a weird voice, through closed lips, swearing and blaspheming.

In the summer of 1688, there was *another* strange event in Massachusetts. The children of a Boston stonemason started having fits, following an encounter with a suspected witch. This case aroused the interest of another famous minister, Increase's son, Cotton Mather.

Cotton Mather took the children into his own house to observe them, looking a little like a reporter after a good story. And sure enough, in

1689, he published *Memorable Providences, Relating to Witchcrafts and Possessions*. It was a bestseller.

It described the fits of the children in great detail. Cotton Mather says they would open their mouths so wide that they dislocated their jaws, and at other times snap their jaws together like a trap. They would stick out their tongues, stretch the joints of their shoulders, elbows and wrists. Sometimes they would force themselves into a ball, at other times, arch their backs "to such a degree that it was feared the very skin of their bellies would have cracked."

They would cry out that they were being cut with knives or being hit. Their necks would appear to be broken and then miraculously mended. Their "heads would be twisted almost around." This bizarre behaviour was going to become horribly familiar to the people of Salem Village.

"Go tell Mankind," Cotton Mather says in the introduction to *Memorable Providences*.

"Go tell Mankind that there are devils and witches…" Samuel Parris did not have many books in the parsonage, but *Memorable Providences* was one of them.

Mary Sibley, one of Parris's neighbours, decides to get involved. Why not try a little *white* magic, she says, and sets about getting Parris's slaves, Tituba and John Indian, to bake a "witch cake". A vital ingredient of this witch cake is going to be urine from the two girls. When it is baked it must be fed to the dog. If the dog acts strangely too, then it is witchcraft for sure.

But if this is supposed to help matters, it certainly does not. In fact, things begin to snowball. Other girls from the neighbourhood had been involved in these fortune-telling sessions and now they too begin showing the same terrible symptoms.

There is Mercy Lewis, seventeen years old and orphaned by the Indian war of 1675; Elizabeth Hubbard, also seventeen, and the niece of Dr Griggs; Mary Walcott, again seventeen, a near neighbour of Betty and Abigail; and there is Ann Putnam.

Ann is the twelve-year-old daughter of local bigwig Thomas Putnam. The Putnam family are staunch Puritans and are engaged in a bitter power struggle with other local landowners. They want Salem Village to become an independent town – and they want the power that will come with it.

The Putnams' support of pastor Samuel Parris has only made him more unpopular. With their help, Parris has become the owner of the village parsonage, rather than just its occupier. The villagers are not impressed, and, as with Parris's predecessors, they stop paying the taxes that provide for the minister's income.

Perhaps the hostility makes Parris nervous, because he decides to call in some local worthies. These include the neighbouring ministers, John Hale of Beverley and Nicholas Noyes of Salem Town. They all agree that Satan is definitely involved, but they tell Parris to pray and have some patience to see what will happen over time.

Just to be on the safe side, though, they also question Parris's slave, Tituba. Abigail and Betty have been saying that she appears to them in visions, pricking and pinching them. Tituba is terrified. She is in real danger: a woman, an Indian, a slave – she is the lowest of the low here, and witchcraft can carry a death sentence. She denies being a witch, but she admits to baking the witch cake.

Under pressure from the ministers, Tituba says the witch cake was her idea: that she heard about it from her old mistress in Barbados. She says that her old mistress was a witch and taught her some tricks to discover witches and to guard against witchcraft.

In years to come, people will say that this witch cake is something to do with voodoo or some kind of tribal magic Tituba picked up in Barbados. But Tituba is an Indian, not an African; her native culture no doubt had magical beliefs, but the witch cake idea was just as likely to have come from England, a country with a rich history of folk magic performed by "cunning men" and "wise women".

There was a belief in England that by boiling or baking the victim's urine, the offending witch would not be able to urinate and would then be easy to spot because of the discomfort he or she would suffer as a result. These villagers did not need Tituba to tell them about magic. They knew all about it for themselves.

But whether it was Tituba's or Mary Sibley's idea, if Tituba can be made to confess to being a witch, then perhaps the whole thing can be sorted out quickly and neatly. So the Reverend Samuel Parris beats the living daylights out of his slave in an effort to get her to confess, but Tituba refuses to be the scapegoat.

Then the afflicted girls scream out that there are two others hurting them. They call out the names of two villagers: Goody Good and Goody Osborne – Goody being short for Goodwife –

and the Putnams file a complaint against Tituba,
Good and Osborne with the Salem magistrates.
There is no police force to pursue a conviction
against suspected criminals; it is left to individuals
to bring charges. A warrant is issued for their
arrest on 1 March. The witch hunt has begun.

Chapter 3

The Afflicted Girls

The authorities plan to hold the pre-trial examinations in Ingersoll's Tavern. This may seem a little strange for Puritans, but village meetings are often held there – it is warmer than the meetinghouse, for a start. Puritans are not against drinking – everyone including children drinks beer (it is safer than water) – it is *drunkenness* that offends them.

However, as soon as the magistrates see the size of the crowd milling around outside, it becomes clear that this is not going to work and they switch venues to the nearby meetinghouse. Not a lot happens in Salem Village and the possibility of a witch trial is too good to miss. The meeting-house is packed to the rafters. This is not a church meeting, this is a public meeting; no sitting in stiff obedience today. This is an altogether more rowdy affair.

At the front of the hall are the magistrates, John Hathorne and Jonathan Corwin. These men come from respected Massachusetts families. They are busy and successful merchants and they have fine white lace at their throats and at their cuffs. They are also hardline Puritans and neither has any legal training whatsoever.

Thirty-seven-year-old Sarah Good is from the other end of Massachusetts society entirely. Sarah has had a sad life. She has not always been poor; her father was a successful innkeeper, but drowned himself when Sarah was only 17. As if that was not bad enough, she lost her inheritance to her mother's new husband.

Sarah Good and her shiftless husband William have been forced to sell their land and are homeless, reduced to relying on the charity of their neighbours. But begging does not suit Sarah and she is quick with a curse if she does not get what she wants. There is no shortage of people

willing to testify to her bad mouth and
disgruntled mutterings. Sarah Good is like a
caricature of a witch, frowning and grumbling.
She even smokes a pipe!

Sarah is brought forward to stand in front of
the magistrates, hemmed in, constables at her
side. The "afflicted girls" – Ann Putnam, Abigail
Williams, Elizabeth Hubbard and Betty Parris –
stand nearby as if part of the court. There is a
hush of expectation as John Hathorne asks his
first question:

"Sarah Good, what evil spirit have you
familiarity with?" Good says she has none. There
are murmurs of disbelief.

"Have you made no contract with the devil?"
insists Hathorne.

"No," answers Good. More muttering.

"Why do you hurt these children?" asks
Hathorne.

"I do not hurt them," says Good. "I scorn it."
She looks around for a friendly face, but she has
no friends here.

"Who do you employ then to do it?" Hathorne is asking her if she has a "familiar" who does these things for her, and Good knows it.

"No creature," she says, and tells them she is falsely accused. Hathorne continues with his questions. When Good denies that she went away from Parris's house muttering under her breath, he starts all over again.

"Have you made no contract with the devil?" he asks again.

"No," answers Good again.

Then Hathorne asks the children to look at Sarah Good and say whether this was the person who had hurt them. The girls look at Good and immediately begin screaming and yelling, scratching at the air, clutching at their clothes, twisting their faces and contorting their bodies. Now it starts.

For many people in the meetinghouse, this is their first glimpse of the afflicted girls' fits. The girls strain their heads round on their necks, they stretch their arms as if they are dislocated from their sockets. They hiss and snarl and stick out their tongues. It could not be further removed from the expected behaviour of a Puritan maid.

"Sarah Good, do you not see now what you have done?" he says over the din. "Why have you not told us the truth? Why do you thus torment these poor children?"

Good, like everyone else, is still reeling from the sight and sound of the afflicted girls' fits, but once again denies the charge. Hathorne again asks her who she "employs" then, and Good, again, says she employs nobody. Hathorne asks her to explain how it was, that the girls came to be tormented. Good is beginning to crack.

"Osborne," she says. "It was Osborne." Success! Hathorne has got Sarah Good to name Sarah Osborne as a witch. He immediately goes back to work on Good. What exactly is it that she mutters as she walks away from people's houses?

"If I must tell, I will," says Good, clearly trying to think of something. Nothing comes.

"Do tell us then," says Hathorne.

"If I must tell I will tell," she says again. "It is the commandments." Then she adds, with a little of the temper that had brought her here in the first place. "I may say my commandments I hope." Hathorne is not impressed.

"What commandment is it?" Bravado turns to panic.

"If I must tell you I will tell you," says Good again. "It is a psalm." She doesn't know her commandments from her psalms. The crowd mutters. *She doesn't even know her commandments from her psalms*. Hathorne has her cornered.

"What psalm?"

There is a deathly silence. *What psalm?* Birds twitter in the trees outside. *What psalm?* Good has nowhere else to go. After a while she makes a feeble effort at reciting some half-remembered psalm. The crowd tut and heckle. The afflicted girls squeal and shriek. *She doesn't even know a psalm!*

And as if things are not bad enough for Good, her own husband is against her. Asked for his opinion, he tells the examiners that he is afraid that his wife "either *was* a witch or would be one very quickly." Goodman Good has to admit that he hasn't actually *seen* his wife do anything "in this nature". It is her "bad carriage" – her bad attitude – to him he explains.

"She is an enemy to all good," the court recorder notes him saying. But maybe it is, "She is an enemy to old Good," that he says. The afflicted make so much noise it is hard to hear. Sarah Good is led away.

Sarah Osborne is next. Just like Sarah Good, Sarah Osborne's life has not been easy. She too was well off at one time, married to a prosperous farmer; but when he died, she caused a scandal by paying off the "indenture" – the contract that tied him to his master – of a young Irish servant. And then marrying him! But now she is old and bed-ridden.

Osborne has also made the mistake of getting on the wrong side of the Putnams when she contested a will and tried to gain ownership of the land that had been left in trust to her sons; sons who just happened to be John Putnam's nephews.

Hathorne begins his questioning in the same way as he did with Good, asking her if she had made a contract with the devil. Osborne says no. He then asks her about Good and about how well she knows her. Osborne falters over the answers, not wanting to be caught in a lie, but not wanting to seem too close to Good either.

"Sarah Good saith it was you that hurt the children," says Hathorne. Osborne says she can't be held responsible if the devil took her likeness and did people harm.

Hathorne asks the girls once again to look at the accused and see if they know her to be the one who hurt them. All of them say it is. All of them go into terrifying fits. Panicked by the screaming and contorting girls, Osborne blurts out that she, too, has been attacked by some kind of devil.

She has been frightened in her sleep. She *saw* or dreamed she saw "a thing like an Indian, all black" which grabbed her by the scruff of the neck and dragged her to the door. The crowd gasp and shudder; with Indian attacks so much in people's minds, Sarah Osborne is probably not the *only* one to have had such a nightmare. But has she not seen anything else?

Sarah Osborne says she has not seen anything else. Several in the crowd shout out that she has. They say they have heard talk about a "lying spirit". Hathorne jumps on this.

"What lying spirit is this?" he says. "Hath the devil ever deceived you and been false to you?" Osborne says it wasn't the devil. It was a voice. A voice she thought she heard – a voice in her head. And what did the voice say?

"That I should go no more to meeting, but I said I would, and did go the next Sabbath day."

When Hathorne asks for information on her

attendance it turns out that she has not been for a year and two months. Sarah Osborne is taken away.

Chapter 4

Tituba the Indian Woman

Tituba is a Caribbean Indian, bought by Parris when he lived in Barbados and brought with him to Boston with another slave called John Indian. Tituba and John were married in 1689 and the Parris family moved to Salem.

Tituba is an Indian in a community that hates and fears Indians. In fact Puritans believe that Indians are servants of the devil, just like witches, or even demons. And Tituba was present during the fortune-telling and a participant in the baking of the witch cake. Even though this is not a trial as such, Tituba must know her life is on the line here. Hathorne gets straight to the point.

"Why did you hurt these poor children? What harm have they done you?" Tituba says they have done her no harm and she has not hurt them at all. Well, says Hathorne, if it is not *her* hurting them, then who is it?

"The devil for all I know," says Tituba. The crowd shift in their seats. Tituba looks nervously from face to face. The *devil*. Maybe it's the devil himself who is hurting them. Maybe the children are possessed, not bewitched.

"The devil come to me and bid me serve him," says Tituba. Children in the gallery lean forward nervously to hear more, hearts pounding.

"Who have you seen?" asks Hathorne. He wants names of other witches.

"Four other women sometimes hurt the children." The villagers shoot fearful glances at their neighbours. *Four other women*. Suddenly it feels much colder.

"Who are they?" asks Hathorne.

"Goody Osborne and Sarah Good," says Tituba. "And I do not know who the others were…" Hathorne asks her what the devil looks like; what shape does he take when he hurts them?

"Like a man, I think," says Tituba. "Yesterday, I being in the lean-to chamber, I saw a thing like a man, that told me to serve him and I told him no, I would do no such thing."

Goody Osborne saw "a thing like an Indian", but Tituba, an Indian herself, is saying the thing she saw just looked "like a man". Hathorne wants to know more about this "thing like a man", this devil. Tituba tells him that the apparition threatened to kill the children, and her, if she did not serve him.

Hathorne asks Tituba if she has seen any other "likenesses" and she says yes, she has seen a hog. And a dog. They wanted her to serve them as well, but again she bravely refused.

"What other creatures have you seen?" asks Hathorne, as if a man, a hog and a dog were not enough. Tituba says she has seen a bird – a little yellow bird – and that the bird lives with "the man who hath pretty things there besides". But has she seen any *other* creatures, Hathorne wonders.

"I saw two cats, one red, another black as big as a little dog," says Tituba.

"What do these cats do?" asks Hathorne, and Tituba tells him that they tell her to serve him. She tells them that they scratched her after prayer because she would not agree to serve him. They make her pinch the children. "I am very sorry for it," she says. They make her do it, she says. They make her go to the Putnam house.

"Who did make you go?" asks Hathorne. Tituba says it is the man; the man and Goody Good and Goody Osborne.

"How did you go?" asks Hathorne. "What do you ride upon?" Tituba has said nothing about riding anywhere on anything, but everyone knows what he is asking.

"I rid upon a stick or pole," says Tituba, to fearful gasps. "And Good and Osborne behind me, we ride taking hold of one another…"

Witches. *Witches*. Witches riding brooms through the night sky to do their evil work; it is an image burned into the minds of everyone here since they were children. The crowd murmurs. So it is true. It is *true*. There is witchcraft in Salem Village.

Tituba accuses Good and Osborne of telling her to kill Ann Putnam; of wanting her to cut Ann Putnam's head off with a knife. The villagers gasp and look at Ann in horror. Hathorne asks Tituba if she had ever practised witchcraft in her own country.

"No," she says. "Never before now." She says she has seen Goody Good with the yellow bird and a cat. Then he asks Tituba what creature Osborne has with her…

"Something," she says. "I don't know what it is. I can't name it. I don't know how it looks. She has two of them," she says, before finally coming up with: "One of them has wings and two legs and a head like a woman." The crowd murmurs, the afflicted wail. The creatures of hell seem to be tumbling out into Salem Village.

"What is the other thing that Good Osborne hath?" asks Hathorne as the noise subsides.

"A thing all over hairy," she says. "All the face hairy and a long nose and I don't know what it is. I can't name it, I don't know how it looks. She hath two of them. One had wings and two legs…" The crowd stare at her open-mouthed. "It goeth upright like a man and last night it stood before the fire in Mr Parris's hall." The girls shriek and flail about. The villagers look at each other, horror struck; fearful of the next revelation, but rooted to their seats as if spellbound.

The image is burned into their minds: a winged demon standing silhouetted in front of the crackling flames of the minister's hearth as if it were the fires of hell itself! Parris's heart must be pounding more than most. After all, it seems that the parsonage is the focus for this evil. Hathorne keeps his composure and calmly moves from Tituba's winged demon to "the thing like a man" she mentioned earlier.

"What clothes does the man appear to you in?"

"Black clothes," says Tituba. There are sharp

intakes of breath and nods of recognition. *Everybody* knows the devil wears black. But then so do many men. And what about the women? What clothes do they wear?

"A black silk hood with white silk hood under it," she says. Ah, silk. Fine clothes. More nods from the crowd. Fine clothes are another temptation of the devil. Tituba says she has seen the woman in Boston when she used to live there. When she tells them what the other was wearing, the girls go berserk, contorting themselves and screaming out in agony. The examiners ask Tituba who it is that is hurting the children and quick as a flash she answers, "Goody Good," and the girls echo her. "Goody Good! Goody Good!" and scream in agony.

Elizabeth Hubbard seems to be the worst afflicted of the girls. When she is asked who is hurting her she goes into an even wilder fit than before. Tituba tells the examiners that the witches have blinded Elizabeth to prevent her from seeing, and then she herself seems to have episodes of being struck dumb. Tituba appears almost to be acting as an interpreter for the girls. It does not stop her from being packed off to jail, though, along with the two Sarahs, Good and Osborne.

And so there it is. A coven of three witches. Bad-mouthed Sarah Good, confused Sarah Osborne, and Tituba, an Indian and a slave. There are few in Salem who are going to miss *them*.

But wait a minute: didn't Tituba say she saw *four* witches?

Chapter 5

Martha Cory

Salem Village is in turmoil. Neighbours eye each other suspiciously. Who will be the next to be afflicted? Who will be the next to be accused? The feuds that have plagued the village for the last fifty years only add to the growing paranoia.

Suddenly *everybody* is seeing witches and strange apparitions. On 1 March, the evening after Tituba's confession, the household of Dr Griggs is sent into a panic when Elizabeth Hubbard, one of the afflicted girls, says she can see Sarah Good – or rather her spectre – standing on the table.

The same evening, a young man says he sees a "strange and unusual beast" which vanishes only to be replaced by two or three women – he took them to be the two Sarahs and Tituba – who "swiftly vanished away". On 2 March, someone sees Sarah Good in his bedroom carrying a strange light. Another man is followed by a big white dog and then later is visited in bed by a grey cat.

Who knows what other nightmares stalk the good people of Salem Village? These wooden houses with their tiny windows are cold and dark even in the daytime, full of shadowy corners and strange creaks. Away from the fire glow or candlelight, *anything* seems possible.

On 11 March, Parris decides to call in those local ministers again, and some of his neighbours, for another day of fasting and prayer. To be on the safe side, he also decides to get his daughter away from all this. Whether he does it out of love or to save himself further embarrassment, we cannot know, but he sends Betty to stay with friends in Salem Town.

On Saturday 12 March, 65-year-old Martha Cory answers the door to two stern-looking men from Salem Village; one is Edward Putnam, Ann's uncle. Martha smiles and coolly tells them that she knows why they have come. The afflicted girls have named her as a witch.

Now Martha Cory is a very different woman from the others named by the afflicted. Martha is clever and quick-witted, a prosperous farmer's wife – and a church member. But she does have a skeleton in her closet. She once gave birth to an illegitimate child – an illegitimate *black* child.

The two men say that Ann Putnam accuses Martha Cory's spectre of hurting her. Martha asks if Ann told them what clothes she is wearing, and it just so happens that the men did in fact ask Ann just that, as a way of confirming her story. And what did she say? Ann answered that the spectre had "blinded" her, so she could not tell. Martha Cory smiles.

The men do not like Martha's attitude. After listening to their lecture about what a terrible thing it is to see a church member accused of witchcraft, Martha decides that attack is the best form of defence. On Monday 14 March, she goes round to Thomas Putnam's house to have it out with Ann. It is a mistake.

As soon as Martha arrives at the door, Ann and the Putnams' 17-year-old servant Mercy Lewis, both collapse into fits, twitching and gibbering. Ann yells that she can see Tituba's yellow bird suckling between Martha's fingers. Martha tries to defend herself but cannot make herself heard. She has no option but to leave.

Then, four days later, Ann Putnam's mother *also* complains of being tortured by Martha. She says that she had been taking a rest from looking after Ann, when she suddenly had a feeling as though she was being "pressed and choked to death".

It is no surprise if Ann Putnam Senior is suffering chest pains, considering the stress of seeing her daughter "bewitched", but it seems as though this is no *ordinary* illness. Ann Putnam says that Martha Cory's spectre is torturing her; torturing her and trying to force her to sign a red book. A warrant is issued for Martha's arrest the very next day.

On this very same day, Deodat Lawson rides into Salem Village from Boston, invited in by Samuel Parris. He was Parris's predecessor as minister, so he knows the village and its infighting. Even so, he must be amazed by what he finds.

Deodat Lawson goes to Ingersoll's Tavern and takes his things up to his room. Suddenly, 17-year-old Mary Walcott appears in his doorway. We can imagine that having a teenage girl in his room probably makes the Puritan pastor just a little nervous.

They talk for a while, but just as she is about to leave, Mary screams and grabs her wrist. The shocked pastor leads her over to the candle. By its flickering light he is horrified to see the fresh imprint of human teeth clearly marking the flesh of her arm.

And it does not stop there. When Deodat Lawson pays a visit to Samuel Parris's house that

same evening, Abigail Williams cries out that she
can see another spectre. But this is not Sarah
Good or Sarah Osborne; this is the spectre of
Rebecca Nurse, a 71-year-old steadfast church
member. Surely she cannot be seeing Goodwife
Nurse? But it seems that Ann Putnam has already
seen Rebecca's spectre sitting in her
grandmother's chair five days earlier.

Abigail persists. "Do you not see her?" she
shouts. "Why, there she stands." Deodat Lawson
and the others stare at where she points, straining
their eyes to see what she sees, but of course they
see nothing. The spectre wants Abigail to sign a
book. "I won't, I won't!" she shouts. "It is the
devil's book for all I know!"

Then Abigail runs crazily into the hearth,
yelling and shrieking, tossing burning sticks out
of the fireplace and scrabbling like an animal to
the fireback as if she is trying to escape up the
chimney. Lawson stares on in amazement. What
on earth is happening here?

So Deodat Lawson can be forgiven for looking a little troubled the following day when he climbs the pulpit to conduct the Sunday service in the meetinghouse. The warrant for the arrest of Martha Cory cannot be enforced because today is the Sabbath, but she is not the type to hide. She decides to come to church and confront her accusers. Ann Putnam and the others go crazy as soon as they see her, screaming and hissing, twisting their faces in agony.

This is the first time Lawson has experienced this shocking display and not surprisingly, he finds it difficult to get through the prayer. And things get worse. When the congregation has finished singing the psalm, Abigail Williams shouts out at him, "Now stand up, and name your text!" and when he has finished reading, she calls out cheekily, "It is a long text."

For these meek Puritan girls to heckle their minister is as shocking as any of their famous fits. There can be no greater evidence that Satan is in their midst than this display of rebellion.

The afflicted girls disrupt the sermon with their riotous behaviour, and Abigail Williams yells out that she can see Martha Cory's spectre sitting on a beam, "suckling her yellow bird between her fingers." Everyone looks up to where she points. But of course only the afflicted can see her.

Martha Cory's examination is set for 12 o'clock on Monday 21 March and after the extraordinary goings-on of the day before, the meetinghouse is packed. Parris is taking the notes now, and portly Nicholas Noyes of Salem Town reads the prayer.

Martha is brought in front of the magistrates and the afflicted are immediately gripped by violent seizures – and there are nine of them now; not just the girls, but four older married women as well, one of them being Ann Putnam's mother, Ann Putnam Senior. Above the din of the afflicted, Martha asks that she be allowed to say a prayer.

"We do not send for you to go to prayer," says Hathorne impatiently. "But tell me why do you hurt these?" pointing to the afflicted.

"I am an innocent person," protests Martha. "I never had to do with witchcraft since I was born. I am a gospel woman."

"Ah! You are a gospel *witch*!" shouts one of the girls. Martha says her prayer anyway, without Hathorne's permission.

"The Lord open the eyes of the magistrates and ministers: the Lord show his power to discover the guilty."

"Tell us who hurts these children," says Hathorne, continuing to use the word children, ignoring the older women. Martha says she does not know. How was it then that she knew in advance that Ann Putnam had been asked what clothes she was wearing?

Martha tries to explain that her husband, Giles, told her that the girls always speak about what the accused witches wear. But as in the case of Sarah Good, a cantankerous wife is about to get her comeuppance. When 80-year-old Giles Cory is asked if Martha was telling the truth, he denies it. A few days later he gives a rambling testimony hinting that Martha might indeed be a witch.

The court hears how Martha took the saddle from Giles's horse to stop him going to the meetinghouse for the examinations of Good, Osborne and Tituba. She had not seen "any benefit" in Giles going, she says. The crowd murmurs. No benefit? No benefit in seeing witches brought to justice?

Hathorne asks her how she knew why Putnam and Cheever had come to her house. She says she had heard that the children were accusing her. Hathorne asks again how she could *know* why they came. Martha falters and says, "I did *think* so."

"But you said you *knew* so," bullies Hathorne, as the girls begin screaming again and complaining that Martha's spectre is biting and pinching them.

Now Mary Walcott and Abigail Williams shout out that they see a black man whispering in Martha's ear.

When they say "black man", they mean black like a shadow, black like a silhouette, black like the night in human form. They mean the devil. Hathorne asks Martha what she has to say about this latest revelation.

"We must not believe all these distracted children say," she says. Hathorne asks her if she believes the girls to be bewitched.

"They may be for ought I know," she says. "*I* have no hand in it." For all his bullying, Hathorne is getting nowhere and Martha continues to deny everything he charges her with.

"Did you not say you would open our eyes?" he asks. Martha lets out another bitter laugh.

The girls' frenzy increases. They mimic Martha's movements. If she clasps her hands together, they call out that *their* hands are being pinched. They show bite marks and fingernail marks to the magistrates and to the crowd.

The afflicted Mrs Pope shouts that her bowels are being ripped out and throws her shoe, hitting Martha on the head. When Martha moves her feet, the girls stamp theirs – STAMP, STAMP, STAMP – and ask her why she did not "join the company of witches massed before the meeting-house." STAMP, STAMP, STAMP... "Did she not know the drum beat?" STAMP, STAMP, STAMP. They shout out that the yellow bird is suckling between her fingers. STAMP, STAMP, STAMP.

The girls yell at Martha that she is bound to the devil for ten years. They shout that she has served six and there are four more to come. Martha Cory is sent to Salem Prison to await trial.

Chapter 6

Rebecca Nurse

Deodat Lawson decides to pay a visit to Thomas Putnam, Ann Putnam's father. Ann's mother, Ann Putnam Senior, has been complaining of being tortured for days. To start with it was Martha Cory who had been pinching and biting her. Now Mrs Putnam has made the even more shocking accusation that the spectre of 71-year-old Rebecca Nurse is tormenting her.

To Lawson's amazement, Rebecca's spectre appears in her nightgown and cap and, just as Abigail said earlier, tries to force her to sign a "red book". Lawson cannot see her of course – but he is in no doubt that she is there, and when Abigail refuses to sign, the spectre tortures her. With Lawson staring on in horror, Ann Putnam Senior pleads with the spectral Rebecca Nurse to leave poor Abigail alone.

An arrest warrant is issued against Rebecca Nurse, who has been ill for some time, and she is brought in front of Hathorne and Corwin in the meetinghouse the following day. Ann Putnam Senior has a fit as soon as Rebecca walks in, and the other afflicted join her. Hathorne asks Rebecca what she has to say for herself.

"I can say before my eternal father I am innocent," says Rebecca.

Ann Putnam Senior yells out wildly, "Did you not bring the black man with you? Did you not bid me tempt God and die?" The crowd gasp, shocked both by Mrs Putnam's outspoken behaviour and by the accusation that Rebecca Nurse had tried to get her to kill herself. Suicide is a terrible sin to these people.

"Do you not see these afflicted persons and hear them accuse you?" says Hathorne.

"The Lord knows I have not hurt them," says Rebecca. "I am an innocent person."

Hathorne asks Rebecca how she can stand there with "dry eyes" while the girls are in such agonies.

"You do not know my heart," says Rebecca. Hathorne casts doubt on whether she has really been ill at all. Maybe she has just been hiding away.

"I am sick at my stomach," says Rebecca. Maybe she means sick *to* her stomach, sick to her stomach with this madness that has taken hold of her village. Maybe she has been hiding away because she has seen all this before and knows where it leads.

Forty-seven years earlier, in 1645, when Rebecca was 24, she lived in Great Yarmouth in Norfolk, England. She was Rebecca Towne then and her father, William Towne, was a local Puritan and member of the Nonconformist church there.

In that year, the corporation of Great Yarmouth invited Mathew Hopkins, the self-styled Witch-Finder General, to search for witches there. Hopkins and his assistant, John Stearne, were on a witch-hunting crusade in which two hundred "witches" would die. Mathew Hopkins "discovered" sixteen witches in Great Yarmouth, all of whom apparently confessed. Just like the Puritans of New England, Hopkins was obsessed by the idea of a contract between these witches and Satan.

This witch craze took place across the English counties of East Anglia – Suffolk, Norfolk, Essex and Cambridgeshire – where so many of the Massachusetts settlers originally hailed from. The Towne sisters themselves emigrated to America in 1649 and married, and they all now live in Salem Village, as Rebecca Nurse, Mary Easty and Sarah Cloyce.

The Townes are one of those families that the Putnams had pushed around back at the start of Salem Village. The feud is very much alive, with an ongoing struggle between the Putnams and the Nurses, Eastys and Cloyces.

Under Hopkins's examination, one of those accused in Great Yarmouth in 1645 said that she heard a knock at her door and when she looked out of the window, there was a "tall, black man" standing outside. Back in the meetinghouse in Salem Village, the afflicted girls have once again claimed to see a very similar black man whispering in Rebecca's ear. Hathorne asks her what she has to say.

"It is false," she says. "I am clear." She means innocent – clear of guilt. Had she not perhaps even been *tempted* to become a witch?

"I have not," says Rebecca firmly. Hathorne asks Rebecca if she thinks the afflicted are pretending then.

"I cannot tell," she says.

"That is strange, everyone can judge," says Hathorne looking at the crowd. The crowd mutters and grumbles in agreement.

"Do you think these suffer against their wills or not?" says Hathorne.

"I do not think these suffer against their wills," says Rebecca.

"Do you believe these persons are bewitched?"

says Hathorne again. Finally, Rebecca gives in and says that she does.

Hathorne softens his tone. Maybe, he suggests, maybe, it was her *apparition* who did the hurting and not her?

"Would you have me bely myself?" says Rebecca. Is he asking her to lie?

As Rebecca speaks, she holds her head to one side. Elizabeth Hubbard cranes her neck to one side and Abigail Williams shouts out for them to lift "Goody Nurse's" head up or Elizabeth's neck will be broken. Sure enough, when they straighten Rebecca's neck, Elizabeth Hubbard's is "immediately righted". Rebecca is sent to jail.

But Rebecca is not the only suspected witch to be examined that day. Dorcas Good was arrested that same morning. She is Sarah Good's daughter. When she looks at the afflicted they yell and complain that her spectre is tormenting them. They even show the magistrate the bite marks.

Hathorne and Corwin go to see her in prison two days later, along with the minister of Salem

Town. She tells them that she has a little snake that suckles on her forefinger. She points to the knuckle and they see a deep red spot about the size of a fleabite. She says her mother gave it to her. Ah, yet more evidence of witchcraft!

Dorcas Good is four-and-a-half years old.

Chapter 7

Samuel Parris

O n the following Sunday, 27 March 1692,
39-year-old Reverend Parris climbs up into
the pulpit. It is spring now, but it is still cold in
this unheated meetinghouse. Parris looks out into
the eyes of his troubled congregation, his long
pale face framed by his shoulder-length hair.

There at the front are his sponsors, the
Putnams, looking to him to take a firm line.
Beyond them, the villagers' faces look up at him,
grim and tense. He must have mixed feelings
about the present troubles. After all, only last
November he was forced to complain that he
did not have enough wood to burn in the
parsonage, and all because members of this
very congregation were refusing to pay the taxes
needed for his upkeep. Now it is different, he
thinks. Now they need me.

Such shocking disregard for their pastor has played straight into the hands of Satan, Parris believes, not considering that his own arrogance or greed may be responsible for his unpopularity.

His sermon today, he tells them, is entitled, "Christ Knows How Many Devils There Are in His Churches, and Who They Are." And his text is John 6:70: "Have I not chosen you twelve, and one of you is a devil?".

If Christ could not tell a devil from a worthy disciple, then what hope do the people of Salem have? But Parris just wants to drive home the point that a witch could be anywhere and any*one*; even someone like Rebecca Nurse.

Rebecca's sister, Sarah Cloyce, can see exactly where the sermon is leading. She gets up and stomps out of the meetinghouse. As she leaves, the wind catches the door and crashes it shut. Parris watches her go, waits for the murmuring to subside, and returns to his sermon.

Parris has already given Mary Sibley a telling off in his office, but after the service he holds a meeting of church members about the witch cake business. Since Mary's tinkering with so-called white magic – "going to the devil, for help against the devil," Parris calls it – all hell has broken loose. There have been "apparitions" and "much mischief". Mary Sibley squirms and hangs her head in shame.

"By these means," says Parris, his voice full of dread, "the devil hath been raised amongst us." There are gasps. "And his rage is vehement and terrible, and when he shall be silenced, the Lord only knows." If anyone is looking to Parris for comfort, they are disappointed.

But Samuel Parris is prepared to give Mary Sibley the benefit of the doubt. She did what she did out of ignorance, and he sees no reason why she cannot carry on being a church member so long as she says sorry. Everyone agrees.

Sarah Cloyce, though, is not so lucky. Two days after her angry exit during Parris's sermon, the afflicted girls claim they see Sarah taking part in a ceremony in the pasture next to the Parris house; a kind of satanic version of holy communion.

Scepticism is dangerous in Salem Village. Doubt itself is a cause for suspicion. Why would you have sympathy for an accused witch? Why would the girls lie? What have you got to fear? What have you got to hide? But there are sceptics, even so.

John Proctor, a successful farmer and innkeeper, bumps into his neighbour, Samuel Sibley, husband of Mary, who baked the witch cake. They meet on the road into Salem Village and they get talking about the examinations of the day before. John's servant, Mary Warren, was part of the group of afflicted girls and John makes it quite clear what he thought about it.

He says that if the girls were left to say what they liked, before long the whole neighbourhood would be full of alleged witches and devils. The girls should all be whipped, he says, and that is exactly what he plans to do with Mary Warren when he brings her home.

John Proctor threatened to give Mary Warren a thrashing the very first time she had a fit and she immediately stopped. She only started again when he was out the following day. And although we might not agree with the idea of whipping Mary Warren, it does seem a bit suspicious that the threat of it could "cure" her. As far as John Proctor is concerned, the afflicted girls are the real criminals.

"Hang them! Hang them!" he shouts. Now whether he means this literally or is saying it for effect we can never know, but given that Samuel Sibley is uncle to Mary Walcott – one of the afflicted girls – this does not seem very wise. The very next day, John's wife Elizabeth – or at least her "spectre" – is biting and pinching Mercy Lewis and demanding that she write in her book. Or so the afflicted girls say...

On 28 March, a couple of young men are having a drink in Ingersoll's Tavern. They spy some of the afflicted girls across the room and one of the men says he has heard that Elizabeth Proctor is going to be examined tomorrow.

Goody Ingersoll says she has heard nothing about Elizabeth Proctor being examined the next day, at which one of the girls cries out, "There is Goody Proctor, there is Goody Proctor, old witch, I'll have her hang." And the rest of the girls join in as usual.

But then a strange thing happens. Goody Ingersoll simply tells them straight out that it is a lie – there is *nothing there*. Realising that neither Goody Ingersoll nor the two men believe them, the girls quickly grin and say they are only kidding. It was "for sport" one of them says. They must have some sport, she says. They must have some sport.

Chapter 8

John and Elizabeth Proctor

It is not until 11 April that Elizabeth Proctor is brought to be examined, along with Rebecca Nurse's younger sister, Sarah Cloyce, who stormed out of the meetinghouse a couple of weeks before.

This time the deputy-governor of Massachusetts himself, Thomas Danforth, is in charge and this time the examination is being held not in Salem Village, but in the meetinghouse in Salem Town. Any hopes of keeping a lid on the witch hunt are gone. This is the biggest show in Massachusetts.

Eighty-seven-year-old Danforth does not even bother talking to the accused. He seems as sure as Hathorne of their guilt. Instead he turns his attention to the "afflicted" and to a new witness, Samuel Parris's slave, John Indian.

John Indian says he is being tormented by two of the accused. Remember, John seems to have had a hand in the baking of the witch cake and his wife Tituba is already in prison. Standing with the afflicted is probably the safest place to be, right now.

"John!" says Danforth. "Tell the truth, who hurt you? Have you been hurt?" John Indian tells Danforth that Goody Proctor and Goody Cloyce brought the "book" to him and choked him.

"Oh you are a grievous liar!" shouts Sarah Cloyce in exasperation.

"She pinched me till the blood came," protests John Indian. Danforth ignores Sarah Cloyce and goes on to another of the afflicted.

"Abigail Williams! Did you see a company at Mr Parris's house eat and drink?" Danforth is "leading" the witness. Instead of asking her what she saw, he is telling her what she saw and asking her to confirm it.

"Yes, Sir," says Abigail Williams. "That was their sacrament."

"How many were there?" he asks.

"About forty," she says. "And Goody Cloyce and Goody Good were their deacons." Forty! *Forty?* The crowd murmur and shift in their seats. Abigail Williams says it was the afflicted girls' blood the witches drank in place of communion wine. They had seen the same thing at Ingersoll's Tavern. Danforth asks her who was there.

"Goody Cloyce, Goody Nurse, Goody Cory and Goody Good." Sarah Cloyce asks for water and collapses. The girls go into spasms, twisting their necks, stretching their joints.

Danforth asks the girls if it is Elizabeth Proctor who is hurting them, but they all seem suddenly struck dumb. Abigail even has her hand stuck in her mouth. When Elizabeth looks at them, they shriek and flail about. Only Mary Walcott is creepily still, held in a trance the whole way through.

Abigail finally takes her hand from her mouth and accuses Elizabeth of sending her spectre to force her to sign the book – the devil's book. Abigail says that Elizabeth told her that the Proctors' maid, Mary Warren, had already signed it. Elizabeth shakes her head.

"Dear child," she says gently. "It is not so." She looks into Abigail's eyes. "There is *another* judgement, dear child." She means God's judgement. She is warning Abigail that she is endangering her soul by telling lies.

Abigail is clearly rattled by this, and immediately yells out that she can see Goody Proctor – her spectre that is – sitting up on one of the beams overhead. The girls join in and the crowd crane their necks to see, though of course, they see nothing.

This is too much for John Proctor. He has a short fuse at the best of times. He is not the kind of man to sit quietly by and watch his wife being accused of dealing with the devil, and all on the say-so of these girls.

He almost certainly shouts out. Maybe he even stands up and threatens the "afflicted". In any event, the afflicted Mrs Pope now claims that she is being attacked by a spectre; but not by the spectre of Elizabeth Proctor – by the spectre of *John* Proctor!

No doubt this enrages John Proctor even more, but his anger plays into their hands. He is like a fish on a hook; the more he struggles, the more surely he is caught. Abigail calls out that John's spectre is coming to torment them, and the afflicted duly go into screams and fits. Instead of helping his wife, John only succeeds in getting himself sent to prison with her.

The Proctors have five children. Being parted from their parents must be terrible enough, but things get even worse. Sheriff Corwin and his men ride round to the Proctors' place. The sheriff's men behave more like a mob, smashing and looting, than an arm of the law. A witch's property is forfeit to the Crown, but no one has been convicted yet, as this brutal sheriff ought to know.

Now it is the turn of the Proctors' servant, Mary Warren. She is examined by John Hathorne back in Salem Village. Abigail Williams accused her of signing the devil's book, remember.

"You were a little while ago an afflicted person," began Hathorne. "Now you are an afflicter. How has this come to pass?" Mary has no real answer.

Elizabeth Hubbard pipes up and tells Hathorne that when Mary stopped having fits, she claimed that the afflicted "did but dissemble" – play-act, in other words. The afflicted girls go wild, howling and twisting themselves into knots. Could anyone really believe this is play-acting?

Elizabeth Hubbard is not worried about introducing the notion that she and the others are lying. She knows perfectly well that Hathorne has no doubts about them. The fact that Mary said the afflicted were lying is going to hurt no one but Mary herself. And Mary knows it too.

So Mary Warren throws a fit herself, shouting out that she will speak, that she will tell, but though the girls scream that she is going to confess, the spectres of Martha Cory and John Proctor "appear" to silence her.

Maybe Mary just does not want to get her master and mistress, John and Elizabeth Proctor, hanged. She is in such a state that she has to be taken out for a while, but her fits start up again when they bring her back. She seems to be stalling for time. But time is running out.

Mary is packed off to jail and when she gets there she reverts to her earlier claim that the afflicted are lying. Mary says that when she was "afflicted", she thought she saw the "apparitions of a hundred persons". Now she is not sure if she has ever seen anything at all.

Chapter 9

Abigail Hobbs

O n 19 April, along with Mary Warren, Abigail Hobbs, Bridget Bishop and Giles Cory are also examined. Eighty-year-old Giles Cory has played a part in sending his wife, Martha, to jail, and by a grim turn of fate he now finds himself one of the accused.

Abigail Hobbs and her family live right on the edge of Salem Village. She is twenty-two and running wild. Even though she has moved to Salem from Casco in Maine – a frontier town plagued by Indian attacks – she seems to have no fear of the woods, and often sleeps out in them at night.

The Hobbs family live on the edge of Salem Village society too. Neither of Abigail's parents are church members and Abigail herself is disobedient, rude and fiery-tempered, given to strange outbursts and bizarre claims. She has even told a friend she "had sold herself body and soul to the old boy" – to the devil, that is. In other words, Abigail Hobbs is a perfect candidate for a witch.

The other accused have dreaded their appearance before the magistrates, but Abigail Hobbs seems to enjoy the attention. She looks up at the stern faces of Hathorne and Corwin and says she has been very wicked. She says she has "seen sights and been scared".

"What sights did you see?" asks Hathorne.

"I have seen dogs and many creatures."

"What dogs do you mean?" asks Hathorne and gives her a little prompting. "*Ordinary* dogs?"

"I mean the devil," says Abigail. It had happened "at the Eastward at Casco Bay." "The Eastward" is what people here call Maine. The devil spoke to her; offered her "fine things" if she did what he asked.

"What would he have you do?" asks Hathorne.

"Why," she says. "He would have me be a witch." The crowd mutter and murmur. So the stories were true. Abigail Hobbs is a witch.

"Would he have you make a covenant with him?" asks Hathorne. Did he want her to make a contract with him?

"Yes," says Abigail. And did she?

"Yes, I did," says Abigail. "But I hope God will forgive me." A confession at last. Hathorne takes Abigail back to the "many creatures" she had mentioned earlier and asks her what they were like. Abigail says one was like a cat and it too had a book and wanted her to sign it. Hathorne asks her if she saw anything else.

"I saw things like men." Abigail says they also told her to sign the book. And had she, asks Hathorne.

"Yes," says Abigail. "One time."

Abigail says that these creatures made a bargain with her, that if she did what they wanted for two years she would be rewarded with fine clothes to wear. Fine clothes again. The plainly dressed crowd tut and shake their heads. And did they give her fine clothes?

"No." Well that just goes to show that you can't trust the devil.

Abigail explains that she is "bid" to hurt Mercy Lewis and Ann Putnam. First she says she pinches them, but then she says it is not her; it is the devil, who pinches them for her. "The devil has my consent."

"Who hurt your mother last Lord's day?" asks Hathorne. Abigail says it wasn't her. It was Goody Wildes from Topsfield. Hathorne asks Abigail again if she visited Salem Village to hurt people and again Abigail says no.

"But you know your shape appeared and hurt people here."

"Yes."

"How did you know?"

"The devil told me, if I gave consent, he would do it in my shape." Abigail seems to have regular chats with the devil. And what shape had the devil appeared in this time?

"Like a black man with a hat."

"Do not some creatures suck your body?" asks Hathorne.

"No," says Abigail.

"Where do they come?" persists Hathorne, ignoring her answer and showing an unpleasant interest in Abigail's body. "To what parts – when they come to your body?"

"They do not come to my body," insists Abigail. "They come only in sight."

"Do they speak to you?" asks Hathorne.

"Yes." How do they speak to her?

"As other folks." Just like anyone else. Even Hathorne finds that a bit hard to take. *Really?* As other folks?

"Yes," says Abigail. "Almost."

This could have probably gone on for hours, but as Hathorne asks more questions Abigail is struck by a convenient attack of deafness. The afflicted girls tell Hathorne that Goody Good and Goody Osborne have put their hands to Abigail's ears. Soon she is "blind" as well.

Then Abigail shouts that the Goods' spectre has told her not to speak, and she is struck by an even more convenient loss of speech. There is little that the examiners can do but have her taken away to prison.

The afflicted girls do not have fits or heckle during Abigail's examination. Abigail is confessing so she is no threat to them. After she is led away, Mercy Lewis, Abigail Williams and Ann Putnam all say how sorry they are for "the condition of poor Abigail Hobbs". The examination notes say that this "compassion" is expressed by the girls "over and over again."

Bridget Bishop comes in next. She receives no such "compassion" from the afflicted girls. Instead they copy Bridget's movements – if she moves her head, they jerk theirs, if she wrings her hands, they squeeze and claw at theirs.

"You are here accused by four or five of hurting them," says Hathorne. "What do you say?"

"I never saw these persons before," says
Bridget. "Nor I never was in this place before."
Why should she have seen them? She lives in
Salem Town, not Salem Village.

Ah, but the girls know *her*. That is, they know
her by reputation. You see, Bridget Bishop has
been up on a witchcraft charge before. Twelve
years ago. She was found innocent, of course. But
there's no smoke without fire, is there? She wears
a bright red bodice too, and has a "smooth
flattering manner", which is just as suspicious to
these grim Puritans as Sarah Good's pipe-smoking
grouch.

And what devilish pranks was Bridget accused
of? Well, it seems that Bridget paid a man
threepence and when he later put his hand in his
pocket, the money had mysteriously disappeared.
Another time, he was driving his cart near Bridget
when it got stuck in a hole. When he got the cart
free, the hole too had mysteriously vanished.

Weak as these accusations may seem, suspicion
clings to poor Bridget and before long every piece

of illness and ill fortune in the neighbourhood is blamed on her. Soon her spectre is sitting on the chests of various Salem men folk, suffocating and choking them and she is being blamed for the fatal illnesses of several children. She is also believed to have killed her first husband by witchcraft.

Bridget denies being a witch. She denies murder. She even says, "I know not what a witch is." She must be the only person in Massachusetts who doesn't. Hathorne jumps at this.

"How can you know you are no witch and yet not know what a witch is?" he says, with devilish ingenuity.

"I am clear," she says – she means innocent – "If I were such a person you should know it."

Suddenly the afflicted Mary Walcott shouts out that her brother Jonathan has struck with a sword at Bridget's spectre and torn her coat. When they check Bridget, they find that her coat is torn. Mind you, it doesn't look much like a *sword* cut – more like a tear, really.

Ah, well, explains Jonathan Walcott, that's because he struck with the sword *still in its scabbard*. Ah! Of course! Everyone nods and agrees that it makes perfect sense. Everyone who wants to escape the dungeons anyway.

And that is exactly where Giles Cory, Abigail Hobbs, Mary Warren and poor Bridget Bishop are headed to await their trials.

On 21 April, nine more suspected witches are examined. But one of the accused, Mary Easty – Rebecca Nurse and Sarah Cloyce's sister – is adamant that she is innocent; *so* adamant in fact that Hathorne feels the need to ask the girls if this is definitely the woman. The girls do not reply at first, but then Ann Putnam and Eizabeth Hubbard suddenly call out:

"Oh, Goody Easty, Goody Easty you *are* the woman, you *are* the woman." And that is good enough for Hathorne. If it comes down to the word of the accused against the word of the afflicted girls, the girls win every time.

But even Hathorne is getting a little concerned that the afflicted girls seem able to recognise the spectres of people they do not know. When another accused witch, Nehemiah Abbott, a 27-year-old weaver from Topsfield, is also absolutely determined that *he* is innocent, Hathorne again checks that the girls are sure.

"Charge him not unless it be he," warns Hathorne, although he has never seen fit to issue this warning before. Some of them say it *is* Nehemiah, but others are not so sure now. Hathorne asks Ann Putnam how she knows his name. Other witches told her, she says. But Mary Walcott says she is not sure and Mary Warren, the most timid of the accusers, says he is definitely *not* the man.

Eventually Hathorne sends accused and accusers outside to get some better light. Now, freed from the suffocating grip of the meeting-house, in the daylight, in the fresh spring air, they are face to face with the young weaver and they lose their nerve.

He is *almost* identical to the spectre, they say, except that the spectre had a wart on the side of his nose. An easy mistake to make. The luckiest man in Massachusetts, Nehemiah Abbott is plucked from the jaws of the witch hunt and set free.

But now busy little Ann Putnam has her most amazing vision yet. A spectre appears who tortures her and wants her to sign his book. The apparition says that he has turned several people to witchcraft, including Abigail Hobbs, that he has killed many soldiers in the Eastward, that he killed Deodat Lawson's wife and child and that he killed his own wives by witchcraft.

The spectre is no one she recognises. Who can this fiend be? She asks him his name and he tells her. Incredibly, it is a one-time pastor of Salem Village: George Burroughs.

Chapter 10

George Burroughs

The witch hunt can take anybody – the very young and the very old, the despised and the respected. Now George Burroughs is about to find that living a hundred miles away is no protection either.

Burroughs was Salem Village's second pastor, and, like all four pastors, he became a butt of infighting in the community. Just as with all the other pastors, the villagers refused to pay taxes for his income.

He was even forced to borrow money from the Putnams to pay for the funeral of his first wife, Hannah. The Putnams had him arrested for debt when he had finally had enough of Salem Village and tried to leave. Burroughs settled up and left, probably hoping never to see the place again.

Burroughs has had an eventful time since he and his family left. He returned to Casco, where he was pastor before Salem Village. It had been destroyed by Indian attacks, but was now being resettled. George Burroughs seems to have thrived in the rebuilt Casco, and Casco seems to have been very content with its pastor. But in 1689, Indians begin attacking once more.

When soldiers arrived to defend Casco, Burroughs was quickly alongside them in a gun battle that saw twenty-one colonists dead and injured, but the town saved. Burroughs was singled out for praise by the commanding officer.

Refugees flooded into Casco. One of them was a fifteen-year-old girl called Mercy Lewis, whose parents had been killed by Indians on nearby Hogg Island. She was placed in the Burroughs's family house as a servant to his wife, three daughters and the four sons born since his return to Casco.

But as the Indian attacks threatened Casco, Burroughs sent Mercy to the relative safety of

Salem Village. This act of kindness would prove to be a big mistake, for Mercy Lewis is now one of the afflicted girls.

Burroughs decided on a move to Wells, further south and better fortified, but before he could make the move, his wife, Sarah, died. Her body was taken to her home town of Salem by ship, and the grief-stricken Burroughs took his seven children to Wells in the spring of 1690.

And not before time. In May, Casco was attacked by Indians trained and commanded by the French. They forced the surrender of the fort and then slaughtered the inhabitants, men, women and children.

But Wells wasn't safe either. On 18 May, the Indians attacked for three days, killing settlers and destroying crops and homes. Burroughs was looked up to here, with his experience of the Indians. And he looked the part – short and powerfully built, with a long mane of pitch-black hair, more like Hawkeye in *Last of the Mohicans* than a Puritan pastor.

Burroughs had shown real heroism, staying on when the surviving ministers had fled to Boston. He had ridden out to preach to frontier villages and fought alongside his parishioners and the soldiers sent to help them. He had co-written letters pleading with Boston for assistance.

How he must have prayed that finally some help would come. But when, on 2 May 1692, Field Marshall John Partridge and his men rode up to his house, it was not to help or congratulate him, but to serve him with a warrant for his arrest. Burroughs was charged with "sundry acts of witchcraft", accused by the afflicted girls of his old parish of Salem Village.

When Burroughs arrives in Salem Village on 4 May, not everyone is convinced of his guilt. A tanner from Salem Town called Elizer Keyser says that he believes that Burroughs is the "ring-leader" of the witches; but Captain Daniel King says he thinks God will clear Burroughs and that if Keyser had doubts about him, then he should be Christian enough to put them to the man himself.

So Keyser, who is related to the Putnams by marriage, reluctantly goes up to the room where Burroughs is being held. Keyser jibbers something about Burroughs staring at him, and when he gets home he says he sees the chimney full of quivering, jelly-like creatures and a weird light.

His maid says she sees them too, but when his wife is called to look, she can't see what either of them is going on about.

George Burroughs is examined on 9 May. Unlike other accused, Burroughs – presumably because he is a minister – is given the chance to answer some questions in private, away from the crazy antics of the "afflicted". He also has a special panel of judges – Hathorne and Corwin are joined by the minister Samuel Sewall, whom Burroughs knows, and William Staunton. It does not go well.

Burroughs makes the shocking admission that he cannot remember the last time he took the sacrament. Then to make matters worse, he admits that only the eldest of his seven children has been baptised.

Burroughs has never been ordained, and therefore cannot conduct Holy Communion. There was only one ordained minister in the whole of Maine and he was killed by Indians in February. And Burroughs did have the excuse of being in a war zone. Maybe Burroughs's frontier life had made these things less important to him anyway. Whatever the reason, this admission only confirms the ministers' bad opinion of him.

The judges also ask him whether it is true that his house in Casco was haunted. Burroughs says it is not, but he did confirm that there were toads. Ah – toads! Just the kind of creature a witch would have as a familiar.

When Burroughs does finally make his entrance into the meetinghouse, the afflicted erupt into screams and spasms, yelling and pulling faces.

It is Burroughs's first view of this extraordinary display and he can't believe his eyes. When asked what he makes of it, he says, "It is a humbling and remarkable providence, but I understand nothing of it."

Mercy Lewis accuses Burroughs – "whom I very well knew" – of tormenting her and trying to get her to sign his book and there are testimonies of Burroughs's alleged superhuman strength: tales of him lifting barrels of molasses and giant muskets. But this is nothing compared to what is to come.

Horribly, Ann Putnam and Susannah Sheldon testify that the ghosts of Hannah and Sarah Burroughs – George's first two wives – appear, accusing George of murdering them. Ann Putnam had been a baby when Hannah died, a toddler when George and Sarah left Salem. How she even knows what any of them look like is a mystery. But it is a mystery the judges are not interested in.

Ann sees the dead wives dressed in their shrouds, ghostly pale. One of them – presumably

Hannah – pulls aside her winding sheet to show Ann the place where Burroughs allegedly stabbed her. The other ghost, presumably Sarah, says Burroughs killed her aboard ship as she travelled to Salem, though in truth she was already dead and her body was being sent home for her funeral.

To make matters even worse, on 3 May, while in prison, Abigail Hobbs's mother, Deliverance, made a new confession in which she says she attended a meeting of witches in the pasture next to the Parris house. A preacher presided over a parody of Holy Communion and told them to "bewitch all in the village, telling them they should do it gradually and not all at once, assuring them they should prevail."

And who was Satan's preacher? Why, none other than the old minister of Salem Village, George Burroughs, of course. It must come as a surprise to no one when the magistrates order that he shall stand trial for witchcraft.

Chapter 11

Well! Burn Me or Hang Me

On 2 May, two days before George Burroughs arrives in Salem Village, another four accused witches are examined and imprisoned. One of them is Susannah Martin. She clearly has no time for the afflicted.

Elizabeth Hubbard and John Indian both say that she has not tortured *them*, but Mercy Lewis falls into a fit and Ann Putnam throws her glove at Susannah who laughs, much to the annoyance of Hathorne. Mercy Lewis cries out again, saying Susannah "hath hurt her many times"; Susannah laughs again.

"Pray what ails these people?" asks Hathorne.

"I don't know," says Susannah.

"But what do you *think* ails them?"

"I do not desire to spend my judgement on it," she says coolly.

"Do you not think they are bewitched?" says Hathorne in disbelief.

"No," says Susannah firmly. "No I do not."

George Jacobs, an old man in his seventies, is examined on 10 May. He is accused by his servant girl Sarah Churchill, who, like Mercy Lewis, has lived in Maine and been orphaned by the Indian wars. "Sarah Churchill accuseth you. There she is," says Hathorne.

George looks at Sarah. He says he has lived in Salem for 33 years, but if she can *prove* he is guilty then he will accept it. Sarah says she was afflicted the night before and Mary Walcott has seen his spectre. George pleads with her, but Hathorne talks over him.

"Look there," he says. "She accuses you to your face."

"What would you have me say?" says George. "I have never wronged a man in word or deed." Hathorne says he has just heard evidence that he *has*. The afflicted girls shriek and howl. George is getting steadily more exasperated. Well, all right then! They can call him a wizard all they like. They may just as well call him a buzzard!

"I have done no harm," says George Jacobs. Sarah Churchill tells Hathorne that George does not pray. George says he cannot read. He is not going to escape that easily. Lots of people can't read or write, but they know their psalms and prayers by heart.

"Well," says Hathorne, "but you may pray for all that. Can you say the Lord's Prayer?"

George stumbles through the prayer and after several goes still can't get it right. The afflicted yell and Hathorne asks Sarah to confirm she saw George's name in the devil's book, and she does. George makes one last attempt to appeal to Hathorne's sense of justice, asking how can Hathorne judge the truth in such a statement –

how can he judge on something that he cannot *know* to be the truth?

"But she *saw* you or your likeness tempt her to write," says Hathorne. What more proof does he need? George Jacobs sees he is wasting his breath.

"Well!" he says finally. "Burn me or hang me, I will stand in the truth of Christ. I know nothing of it."

But George's sixteen-year-old granddaughter Margaret is not so brave. When given the choice between confessing and living, or telling the truth and being hanged, she chooses, as many would, to stay alive. Margaret Jacobs confesses to being a witch, and agrees that her grandfather and George Burroughs are witches too.

And after three weeks in those stinking dungeons, poor Mary Warren also gives in. She says that her old master, John Proctor, gave her the devil's book and makes a detailed testimony against her co-accused, Alice Parker and Ann Pudeator, women she does not even know.

The Mary Warren of April, the Mary who knew the girls to be liars because she had been one of them herself, has gone for good. She will never make that mistake again. Now there are thirty-six accused witches in prison, and the hunt is on for more.

Chapter 12

Gallows Hill

In the middle of May, Sir William Phipps, the new Governor of Massachusetts, sails into Boston harbour on the frigate *Nonesuch* from England. With him is the famous Puritan minister, Increase Mather, and with them, they have Massachusetts's new charter.

This is a mixed blessing for the accused witches. Now the Governor is back, now there is a new charter, there will be less tension; people will know where they stand, and there might even be some order imposed.

On the other hand, up until Sir William returned to New England, the accused witches could only be *examined*, rather than tried, because the legal system had been suspended. All that is about to change.

Now Massachusetts has its new charter, the accused can be tried, and, if found guilty, *they can be hanged.*

Sir William is shocked to find the colony's dungeons filling with accused witches and, in a bit of a panic, he sets up a special court called a Court of Oyer and Terminer. The person he appoints as presiding judge is a staunch Puritan and just as keen a witch-hunter as Hathorne. His name is William Staunton.

The accusations carry on spreading. One of the names "cried out" by the afflicted is Elizabeth Cary, the wife of a wealthy merchant of Charlestown called Nathaniel Cary. Now Nathaniel Cary isn't the type of person to just sit back and wait for the sheriff. Instead, he decides to go to Salem Village and see what all this nonsense is about.

Nathaniel and his wife arrive on 24 May and get a front row seat at the meetinghouse. Cary is hoping to see for himself just how fair these

examinations are. He seems to have no idea of
the danger that he and his wife are in.

The afflicted girls come up, sniffing like wolves,
asking his wife's name. Of course, as they have
already accused her, they should really know who
she is – but then, like many of those they accused,
they have never seen her before in their lives.

Cary arranges a private meeting with the
Reverend John Hale. He had hoped to see him in
Parris's house, but Hale takes him to Ingersoll's
Tavern. In return for some cider, John Indian
shows Cary scars he says are from witchcraft. To
Cary's eyes, though, the scars seem suspiciously
old.

Cary had arranged with Hale to have a private
meeting with Abigail Williams, but instead *all* the
afflicted suddenly "tumble in like swine", as if
they had been listening at the door, and accuse
Elizabeth Cary of being a witch. A warrant is
drawn up and she is hauled in front of Hathorne.

Elizabeth is made to stand with her arms
stretched out. Nathaniel asks if he can hold one

of her hands but is refused. He wipes the tears from her face and, terrified, she asks if she can lean on her husband to stop herself fainting.

"You had strength enough to torment those persons," says Hathorne cruelly. "You have strength enough to stand."

Elizabeth is sent to Boston Prison. Nathaniel manages to get her transferred to Cambridge but she is still loaded down with leg irons as if she was a murderer, and she goes into convulsions. He begs the jailer to take them off, but it does no good.

The General Court orders a day of fasting – across the whole province this time – on 26 May. It does no good. Two days later, the afflicted complain that yet more witches are tormenting them and some of those accused are examined on 31 May in Salem Village.

The afflicted girls are called in by nearby Andover and soon the accusations and confessions are flying. In the Andover meetinghouse, accused witches are made to touch the afflicted girls – the "touch test" it is called.

It works like this: the afflicted are allowed to touch the accused and, if their fits stop, it is seen as a sign that the witch's evil has temporarily flowed back into the witch; proof that the accused really is a witch.

One of those accused is Martha Carrier, another woman with a reputation for witchcraft. Her neighbours blame her for an outbreak of smallpox.

"She looks upon the black man," shouts one of the girls as Martha Carrier is being examined.

"What black man do you see?" Hathorne asks Martha.

"I saw no black man," she says, "but your own presence." *But your own presence!* Is she comparing Hathorne to the devil? Hathorne hits back.

"Can you look on these and not knock them down?" he says. But Martha is having none of this either.

"They will dissemble if I look at them," she says and refuses to look. But the afflicted fall down anyway. "It is false," says Martha to Hathorne. "The devil is a liar. I looked upon none since I came in the room but you." The girls continue to scream and wail.

"It is a shameful thing that you should mind these folks that are out of their wits," says Martha Carrier before being led away to prison. After imprisoning Martha Carrier, John Hathorne examines the Carrier children.

"How long hast thou been a witch?" Hathorne asks Sarah Carrier. Ever since she was six years old, she says.

"How old are you now?" asks Hathorne.

"Near eight year old. Brother Richard says I shall be eight years old November next."

But after sending dozens of supposed witches to prison, the justice of the peace in Andover, Dudley Bradstreet, has had enough and refuses to issue any more warrants. Justice Bradstreet suffers the same fate as everyone who has not given total support for the witch hunt and the afflicted girls.

He and his wife are accused of witchcraft. His brother is even accused of bewitching a dog in Salem Village. Maybe it is the same dog that ate the witch cake all those months ago. The witch hunt is spiralling out of control.

The new Court of Oyer and Terminer gathers a jury and on 31 May nine of the accused witches are ordered to be brought to Salem Town from prison in Boston. The trials begin on 2 June in the courthouse in Salem. The first accused to be brought before the judges is Bridget Bishop.

The trial takes pretty much the same course as the examinations. Bridget stands between two constables about seven or eight feet from the judges, with the afflicted girls between. Bridget is restrained, but the girls are not. They shriek and leap into fits whenever she looks at them.

As before, the afflicted girls mimic Bridget's postures and claim the ghosts of people she had killed are in the courtroom accusing her. As before, neighbours give their testimonies, telling tales of witchcraft, of "poppets" Bridget is supposed to have made out of rags and hog-bristles, stuck all over with pins.

But worst of all, the court is told how, when Bridget was led past Salem meetinghouse on her way to court that very morning, she looked at the building and there was a great crash from inside. When they went to find out what had happened, a large board had seemingly been ripped from the wall and was found across the other side of the room.

With all this "evidence" against her, what could the verdict possibly be, other than guilty as charged? Bridget Bishop is ordered to be executed without delay; she is to be hanged the following Friday.

But one of the judges is not convinced. Nathaniel Saltonstall resigns in protest. Not surprisingly, the afflicted girls promptly accuse him of witchcraft. No one is safe now – *no one*.

On 10 June 1692, Bridget Bishop is brought blinking out of the darkness of Salem Prison into a New England summer's morning, put in a two-wheeled, horse-drawn cart, followed and taunted by a jeering crowd to a craggy hill on the Boston Road and hanged.

But "hanged" seems too gentle a word for it. Her head covered, her arms bound, she is left dangling, kicking, gasping, with a rough hemp rope knotted round her neck, choking to death for ten minutes or more, before being cut down and dumped in a shallow grave.

On 15 June, a pamphlet called the *Return of the Several Ministers Consulted* is delivered to Sir William Phipps. It is believed to be the work of Cotton Mather, and it urges a caution that Mather himself has never shown. It warns that the devil is a trickster and can appear in the shape of an innocent man if he so chooses. Because of this, spectral evidence should not be enough to convict *anyone* on its own.

Cotton Mather says the "touch test" too could be open to devilish trickery, and he also raises questions about the atmosphere that the examinations are carried out in – their "noise, company and openness".

"Nevertheless," Cotton Mather's pamphlet ends, "we cannot but humbly recommend unto the Government the speedy and vigorous prosecution of such as have rendered themselves obnoxious, according to the direction given in the laws of God, and the wholesome statutes of the English nation, for the detection of witchcrafts."

Cotton Mather and the other Boston ministers could choose to slow down the whole witch hunt now. But the truth is they don't want to slow it down. They want "speedy and vigorous" prosecutions. And speedy and vigorous is what they will get.

On 29 June, Sarah Good, Rebecca Nurse, Susannah Martin, Elizabeth Howe and Sarah Wildes stand trial. All the women are forced to

submit to humiliating, intimate body searches.
Their searchers are not after hidden weapons, but
"devil's marks" or "teats" from which familiars
might suckle.

Some people do even have extra nipples, but
most of these so-called teats may in reality be
warts or even pimples. These ignorant and
gullible searchers do not take much convincing.

Susannah Martin, Sarah Good and Alice Parker
do not have anything of interest, but the
searchers manage to find "teats" on the other
three women. Another strip-search is ordered
later in the day and these so-called "teats" have
disappeared. But then that only makes them seem
even *more* unnatural.

Despite the warning in the *Return* about the
"noise, company and openness" of the
examinations, the afflicted are allowed to put on
their usual show for the packed courtroom. As
each of the accused is brought in, the afflicted
girls go through all the screams and seizures and
spasms they went through at the examinations,

and with the same effect. And, despite the warning about the "touch test", it is still used here and the results are used as "evidence".

During Sarah Good's trial, an incident happens that shows just how unquestioning the authorities have become. One of the afflicted yells out that she has been stabbed in the breast. To everyone's amazement, she produces the point of a knife.

However, a man in the crowd speaks up to say that he broke his knife the day before, when the very same afflicted girl was standing nearby. The man shows them the other half of the knife that he still has in his pocket.

When the two pieces are put together, sure enough, they fit perfectly. This is transparent trickery and should warrant some kind of criminal charge in itself. After all, people's lives are at stake here. So what does Judge Staunton do?

Well, the girl is told off for lying, but it does not influence the judge's view of the other girls. In fact it does not even stop that *same* girl from giving more evidence later. The afflicted girls must feel they are untouchable, all-powerful. But they are in for a surprise.

The foreman of the jurors comes back into the crowded courtroom at Rebecca Nurse's trial. When asked what the verdict is, the foreman shocks everyone by saying that the jury find the defendant *not* guilty. There is a pause as this sinks in and then the afflicted react with fits which shock even those who have been watching them for months. It is as if they are exploding with anger at the jury. How dare they go against us? How *dare* they?

Two of the judges say they are not satisfied by the verdict, one walking off the bench, and despite the fact that they have already declared Rebecca not guilty, Staunton asks the jury to think again. Have they, he wonders, given enough thought to Rebecca saying, "What, do you bring her? She is one of us."

Rebecca had said these words when that confessed witch Abigail Hobbs was brought forward to give evidence. Staunton is hinting that Rebecca means one of *us* – one of us *witches*, even though she later wrote a declaration stating that she meant Abigail was a *prisoner* like they were.

The jury foreman asks Rebecca what she meant, but she cannot hear him over the din of the girls' fits. Her silence is enough to change the jury's mind. They change the verdict and she is sentenced to hang. Parris and members of Salem church excommunicate Rebecca on a unanimous vote, that very afternoon.

But Sir William Phipps is persuaded, by friends of Rebecca, or by his own uneasy conscience, to grant her a reprieve. No sooner has he done so than some "Salem gentlemen" persuade him to change his mind, just as Staunton did with the jury. Rebecca is declared guilty once again. Even by the standards of the 17th century, this is hardly justice.

And so, on 19 July, five women – Rebecca Nurse, Sarah Wildes, Susannah Martin, Elizabeth

Howe and Sarah Good – are hanged. They die as they lived. Rebecca Nurse dies praying for forgiveness towards her accusers; Sarah Good dies cursing *hers*. Both insist they are innocent.

The dead are cut down and their bodies shoved into the crevices in the nearby rocks like garbage. They are not buried; simply disposed of. That night, under the cover of darkness, some members of Rebecca's family take her body from the shallow grave on Gallows Hill, and take it home. They bury her in a secret, unmarked grave, trying hard to follow Rebecca's prayer – to forgive the people who have done this wicked thing.

Chapter 13

From the Dungeons in Salem

The number of confessed witches is steadily growing, and, as each witch confesses, she names others. Those named are arrested and examined, those that confess name others in their turn; and so it goes on. Massachusetts must be *full* of witches. After all, no one is making these people confess... Are they?

On 23 July, John Proctor sends a petition to the Puritan ministers of Massachusetts. He is typically defiant. The petition is well argued, but bitter, as if he were spitting the words out between clenched teeth.

He writes of "our case" and "our accusers".

This is not just about himself, this is an attack on the whole process that has seen innocent people jailed and condemned and hanged.

John says that not just the accusers, but the judges and jury were set against them and that "nothing but our innocent blood" will be enough for them, "having condemned us already before our trials."

He writes that, if the devil is involved, then he has set the court against the accused. He says that the "magistrates, ministers, juries, and all the people in general" have been stirred up against them "by the delusion of the devil".

Five confessed witches have just accused John and the others of witchcraft; but these confessions, says John, were not all made willingly. "Two of the five," he says, "are young men, and would not confess anything till they tied them neck and heels till the blood was ready to come out of their noses."

Being tied neck and heels is torture, plain and simple. The victim is laid on his stomach and his body bent upwards until his neck can be tied to his feet and tightened. Now we see why some people have "confessed". Just the fear of being tortured would be enough for some.

John's own son was given this treatment. His torturers would have left him like that, with blood pouring from his nose, for twenty-four hours, had not one of them "more merciful than the rest" taken pity on him and had him released.

The authorities have already taken away their land and property, but, John writes, they will not be satisfied until they have taken their lives. If the trial cannot be moved to Boston, then he begs them to change the magistrates, and to attend the trial so they can see for themselves what is going on. It is a heartfelt and desperate plea, but as far as the ministers are concerned, it is the desperate plea of a *wizard*.

On 5 August, John Proctor, his wife Elizabeth, George Burroughs, John Willard, George Jacobs Senior and Martha Carrier stand trial. When

Martha is told that some of the afflicted have had "their necks twisted near around" by her spectre, she tells them that she does not care if they had them "twisted quite off". And why should she? Those girls are talking her to the gallows.

By far the most important of these so-called witches, in the eyes of the court, is George Burroughs, a minister turned to the devil. They must make a special example of Burroughs. Both Cotton and Increase Mather have come to see *him* tried.

Witnesses again testify to Burroughs's superhuman strength. The afflicted girls and confessed witches are on hand to say that he was the devil's preacher at the meeting outside Parris's house. Elizer Keyser tells the court about the spooky jellies in his chimney and Ann Putnam passes on the testimonies of Burroughs's dead wives. Burroughs is found guilty and condemned to hang. And so are all the other accused.

Margaret Jacobs writes a touching letter "from the dungeon in Salem Prison" to her father, George Jacobs Junior. She tells him that because of bullying by the magistrates and her "own vile and wretched heart", she has confessed to things she knows to be untrue.

Margaret was bullied into lying by Hathorne and Corwin, but eventually her guilty conscience would not let her continue. Margaret has recanted her confession.

She makes a declaration to the court, explaining how she was accused by some of the "possessed persons" of afflicting them. She told the authorities that she had not the slightest idea who afflicted the girls, but she was told that she *must* do, and that if she would not confess, she "would be put down in a dungeon and would be hanged." If on the other hand she confessed, she would have her life. She now tells the court she was frightened into cobbling together a confession, which was "altogether false and untrue."

Immediately after her false confession, she was tormented by a crisis of conscience and could not sleep, fearing that the devil would have her soul for telling lies.

She says that at the time of making her confession she did not even realise that she was swearing to it, and that she had not known what making an oath meant, but she hopes that the Lord will forgive her.

"What I said, was altogether false against my grandfather, and Mr Burroughs, which I did to save my life and to have my liberty", she says. Margaret says that she could see no choice but to deny her confession, "choosing rather death with a quiet conscience, than to live in such horror."

When a confession means freedom and life, and refusing to confess means the stinking disease-ridden dungeon and the gallows, it is surprising that *all* the accused witches do not confess.

But what is Margaret's reward for her honesty, for bravely owning up? She is arrested and hauled off to Salem Prison. Confessing – *falsely*

confessing – bought her freedom, despite the fact
that she was confessing to a crime. Now that she
is denying the crime, she is re-arrested and
imprisoned. She is still a witch in the eyes of the
magistrates, but now one who refuses to admit to
it and seek their forgiveness.

As soon as Margaret Jacobs is re-imprisoned,
she seeks out George Burroughs and asks his
forgiveness for accusing him. Burroughs forgives
her instantly and they pray together in the gloom
of the dungeon.

Meanwhile, on 19 August, those condemned a
fortnight before are loaded into a cart and sent
on their way to Gallows Hill. The only person
not present is Elizabeth Proctor, who is pregnant
and is spared by law, so that the innocent life
she carries will not be taken.

The afflicted girls follow the cart, taunting and
heckling. Crowds fill the streets, jeering and
shouting. Everyone hates a witch. And not only
that; here is one of those self-righteous ministers

caught as a wizard. There must be a secret delight in being able to jeer at a preacher.

And talking of ministers, they all gather like crows to see Burroughs swing – John Hale of Beverley, Nicholas Noyes of Salem Town, Samuel Sewall and, of course, Cotton Mather. But before the hangman does his work, Burroughs makes a speech, and recites the Lord's Prayer – *faultlessly*.

Does this mean that George Burroughs is less of a witch than George Jacobs? – of course not. But a test is a test, and Burroughs has just passed with flying colours. The crowd become restless and look around. The words of the prayer hang in the air. "Deliver us from evil." *Deliver us from evil*. The spell begins to break. They are not so sure after all.

The afflicted girls snap into action. They say "the black man" is dictating to Burroughs. Strange, the devil helping someone to say the Lord's Prayer. But it is enough to convince those who want to be convinced, and George Burroughs is hanged anyway.

Then Cotton Mather speaks out, perhaps sensing that many in the crowd are not happy at the sight of a god-fearing minister hanging from the gallows. Seated on his horse, he reminds them that Burroughs had never been ordained. He is not a *real minister*. Not like Cotton Mather. The hangman is allowed to carry on.

John Proctor pleads for his life, saying he is not ready to die. After all, though his wife is to be spared, he will never see the child she carries. Proctor asks Nicholas Noyes to pray with him and for him but Noyes refuses because Proctor "would not own himself to be a witch". Because Proctor would not confess. Because he would not *lie*.

The hanged are cut down. George Burroughs is dragged and dumped "in a hole or grave, between the rocks, about two foot deep, his shirt and breeches being pulled off, and an old pair of trousers of one of the executed, put on his lower parts..." When the bodies have been heaped in, his hand and chin can still be seen sticking out.

George Burroughs's humiliation is over. The crowd, the ministers, Nicholas Noyes, Cotton Mather, the Putnams, the afflicted girls all turn and head back down the hill into Salem.

On 25 August, a woman called Susannah Post confesses to attending a gathering at which there were 200 witches present, and she says she has heard there are 500 witches in the country. Samuel Parris, ever ready to fan the flames, delivers a sermon saying, "If ever there were witches, men and women in covenant with the devil, here are *multitudes* in New England." The witch hunt roars on.

Chapter 14

More Weight!

Yet more of the accused are brought before the Court of Oyer and Terminer. On 9 September, six women are tried and condemned to die, Martha Cory and Mary Easty among them. But Martha Cory's husband Giles is missing from this group.

Giles Cory was examined back in April. Stubborn by nature, he is refusing to have anything to do with the court. When quizzed by the judges in September he refuses to speak. Maybe he feels that the whole thing is rigged. And he may have a point. Here is Ann Putnam:

"The deposition of Ann Putnam who testifieth that on 13 April 1692, I saw the apparition of Giles Cory come and afflict me urging me to write in his book…" It is the usual damning stuff. But Mercy Lewis seems to have had the *exact* same experience:

"The deposition of Mercy Lewis aged about 19 years who testifieth and saith that on 14 April 1692 I saw the apparition of Giles Cory come and afflict me, urging me to write in his book..."

Are the girls getting their stories to match before making the accusations? Or are they being told what to say? Their testimonies are almost identical.

Maybe Giles Cory just knows a sham when he sees one, and is not going to play ball. It is a legal requirement that the accused enter a plea, but Giles is refusing to say whether he is innocent or not. In fact he is refusing to say anything at all. But there is an old English solution to this. It was called *piene forte et dure*.

On 19 September Giles Cory is taken out of the courthouse, stripped and laid on the ground. The sheriff and his men then put a board across his chest and begin heaping stones on top. He is being "pressed" to enter a plea.

But still the stubborn old farmer will not give them what they want. Legend has it that he is heard to say "More weight! More weight!" but, whether he says it or not, more weight is what he gets. After two days, his rib cage collapses and he is crushed to death.

Cold-hearted Sheriff Corwin shoves the dead man's tongue back into his mouth with the tip of his cane. Surly and eccentric in life, Giles has managed a kind of heroism at his death. He has not "belied" himself.

The horrible manner of Cory's death is shocking, even by the standards of what has gone on before. Some people had hoped that they had left this kind of horror behind in England. Cory might have been a cantankerous old character, but he was a full member of the church, a successful farmer. Where is it all going to end?

But the Putnams are on hand again, to blacken Cory's name even further and justify the old man's death. Ann Putnam's father, Thomas, sends a letter to Judge Samuel Sewall.

"The last night my daughter Ann was grievously tormented by witches, threatening that she should be pressed to death before Giles Cory." Was this a dream – the *guilty* dream – of someone who has seen a man crushed to death on her say-so? Or was Thomas Putnam simply making it up?

Thomas says that everybody seems to have forgotten that, seventeen years earlier, Giles Cory kept a servant who died suddenly, "bruised to death" with blood clots around his heart. Putnam says it had cost Cory "a great deal to get off." Even if Cory wasn't a wizard, Putnam is arguing, he was probably a murderer. So what's all the fuss about? In a way, justice has been served by crushing him to death.

Mary Easty sends a petition addressed to "his excellencies Sir William Phipps: Governor, and to the honoured judges and magistrates." She has suffered the torture of being cleared by the afflicted girls and let out of prison, only to be thrown back inside three days later, when they squealed that she was afflicting them again.

Mary again says that she is innocent, and, knowing how wrongly accused she has been, she is willing to assume that the other accused are innocent as well. It is a painfully sad letter.

"I petition to your honours not for my own life," says Mary, "for I know I must die and my appointed time is set," but she pleads with them that "no more innocent blood" be shed. She begs that the judges show the same scepticism towards the afflicted as they have towards the accused. She asks that they examine the afflicted "strictly, and keep them apart".

Mary has a good point. No one has ever "examined the girls strictly" – the courts have taken everything the afflicted have said and done as the Gospel truth. As to being kept apart, Betty Parris's fits had ended as soon as she was sent away from the other girls. Mary Warren had said that she and the girls were pretending when she was put in prison. Whether they would have all come to their senses – or lost their nerves – if they had been separated, we will never know.

Mary Easty also says that if the judges put some of the *confessing* witches on trial, they might find they changed their tune. She is confident, she says, that, like Margaret Jacobs, "there are several of them has belied themselves."

It may seem incredibly stubborn of Mary Easty to refuse to lie to save her own life, but, to people like Mary and Margaret Jacobs, it was better to die an honest person than endanger their souls with such a terrible lie. No one was going to make Mary say she was in league with Satan; not Hathorne, not Staunton; not the hangman himself.

And the hangman is busy. Eight more board the cart to Gallows Hill at the end of September – including Martha Cory and poor Mary Easty herself. It could have been fifteen… Five are reprieved because they confess, just as Mary Easty had complained. Even Abigail Hobbs, who admitted to having regular talks with Satan, is let off because she confessed and named others. Abigail Faulkner escapes, like Elizabeth Proctor, because she is pregnant.

Again the condemned make moving last speeches from the gallows. Again they declare their innocence. Not surprisingly, Mary Easty's last words are "as serious, religious, distinct and affectionate as could be expressed, drawing tears from the eyes of almost all present." *Almost* all.

When the condemned have all been executed and their limp bodies hang on the gallows, creaking and turning slowly to and fro, Nicholas Noyes, vindictive minister of Salem Town, looks at them in disgust and sneers, "What a sad thing it is to see eight firebrands of hell hanging there."

The crowd begin to move off. The minds of many are troubled. Eight firebrands of hell? Was Mary Easty really a firebrand of hell? Could anyone be *less* like a firebrand of hell?

Chapter 15

Cotton Mather

It is the beginning of October and the forests of New England glow in their autumn colours; maple leaves shimmering red and orange like the dying embers of some huge fire. The colony is still reeling from the recent hangings when Increase Mather delivers a sermon entitled *Cases of Conscience Concerning Evil Spirits Personating Men.*

Far too late, Increase Mather asks himself, "Whether the devil could take the form of an innocent person," and comes to the conclusion that he can. He says the devil can trick the minds of afflicted people and make them believe that even the most pious of people were tormenting them.

Increase says that taking the life of anyone simply because a possessed person accuses them, "will bring the guilt of innocent blood on the land..." This has been said before in the *Return*, but now there is a mood among some in authority to listen.

"It were better," says Increase Mather, "that ten suspected witches should escape, than one innocent person be condemned." These are fine words – words that should have been shouted from the pulpit of Salem Village meetinghouse months ago. Increase Mather's statement is signed by fourteen leading ministers – but not by his son, Cotton Mather.

In *Wonders of the Invisible World*, published this same month, Cotton Mather replies to his father's sermon. "If a drop of innocent blood should be shed in the prosecution of the witchcrafts among us, how unhappy are we!"

"But on the other side," says Cotton Mather, "if the storm of justice do now fall only on the heads of those guilty witches and wretches which have defiled our land, how happy!" Cotton Mather is saying that the accused are *not* innocent, so there is no problem.

Wonders of the Invisible World has been commissioned by Sir William Phipps, to present the trials in a favourable light, and it has a preface by Judge William Staunton. But others take a more critical view.

Joseph Dudley, former deputy-governor of Massachusetts, submits some questions on the subject of spectral evidence to a group of Dutch and French Calvinist ministers. They come to the same conclusion as Increase Mather: that the devil can take the form of even a good man and visit the afflicted in the shape of a spectre, fooling them into thinking that this person is the source of their affliction. It would be a mistake – "the greatest imprudence" – to convict anyone on this kind of evidence alone.

Then a Bostonian merchant, Thomas Brattle, writes an open letter on the subject of the witch hunt. Brattle is also a mathematician and scientist, a member of the Royal Society. He casts doubt on whether it is even possible to try a case of witchcraft. Although it is true, he says, that all kinds of testimonies are heard at the trials about the accused attending witch meetings or performing, "things which could not be done by ordinary natural power", even if ten thousand such pieces of evidence were brought in, how would you *prove* any of them?

And he is right. How could you ever prove that someone is a witch? You could prove that someone *believed* themselves to be a witch, but you could never prove they were capable of supernatural crimes. It comes down to whether you believe them to be a witch and the law requires something more than belief. Or it should.

Brattle says, "the prisoner at the bar is brought in guilty, and condemned, merely on the evidences of the afflicted girls". How could it ever be proved that the girls saw any spectres or were ever tormented by them? The court is just taking their word for it.

Brattle's common sense seems to open a window in that stuffy meetinghouse. Of the fifty-five confessing witches, Brattle says he reckons that thirty of them are possessed and as "afflicted as the children."

And in any case, if witchcraft is such a terrible crime, a crime carrying the death penalty, then why have the authorities not been even-handed with the enforcement of warrants? How is it that the rich manage to buy themselves off and escape punishment? If some can evade the warrant and others not, how can that be called justice?

He has a point. The afflicted girls had long ago accused the rich Salem merchant Philip English, and his wife Mary. They are celebrities. They live in the finest house in Salem, right on the harbour. They have evaded capture.

And when wealthy Nathaniel Cary saw how the trials were being conducted, he knew straight away that his wife did not have a hope in hell of getting out of there alive, so they escaped – first to Rhode Island, and then to New York.

Sir William Phipps has been away in the Eastward fighting the Indians and the French, and returns to find things even worse than when he left. Not only are prisons overflowing, the afflicted girls' accusations are getting ever wilder.

They have accused magistrate John Corwin's mother-in-law, two sons of the former Governor, the wife of Reverend John Hale of Beverley. They have even accused Lady Phipps, Sir William's own wife!

Cotton Mather presents Sir William with the completed *Wonders of the Invisible World*, but the tide is turning against the witch-hunters. Phipps is relieved that the advice from Increase Mather and others may allow him an escape from the mess he himself has helped to make.

The first thing he does is ban the use of spectral evidence. No more, "I saw the apparition of Goody Smith or Jones doing this or that." No more tales of spectres tormenting people or ghosts accusing their "murderers".

On 12 October, Phipps writes to the Privy Council in London saying that he has forbidden any more imprisonments on the charge of witchcraft. On 26 October, the General Court of Massachusetts votes to hold another day of fasting and a meeting of ministers to decide on the best way to proceed.

Finally, on 29 October, five harrowing months after he set it up, Sir William Phipps dissolves the Court of Oyer and Terminer. He prohibits further arrests on the charge of witchcraft and even allows some of the accused out of prison – though only on bail.

Only a few short months ago the afflicted were ordinary village girls, unnoticed, ignored; now they are famous. The well-to-do consult them as if they were wise-women.

The afflicted are called on by the town of Gloucester, further up the coast, to come and use their witch-finding powers on a set of suspects. Sure enough, the girls "discover" four witches, who are all packed off to prison to await trial.

In November, Gloucester calls the afflicted girls back to investigate another suspected witchcraft case. The girls are crossing a bridge on the way to the courtroom when they pass an old woman. All of a sudden, the afflicted come to a halt and are gripped by violent fits, squealing and shrieking, twisting their faces in agony. The old woman must be terrified.

But this time, the onlookers don't take this as a sign that the old woman is a witch. Instead, they seem to see it as a sign of how dangerous the girls have become. They do not look at the old woman. They look at the girls. Autumn leaves drift by on a chill breeze.

The girls are quick to see that their audience is not impressed. They wrap themselves in their cloaks, shoot nervous glances at each other and walk on, doing their best to ignore the cold stares that follow them.

Once in court, the girls are on firmer ground. They are still treated as expert witnesses here. So they tell the court how they have seen spectres sitting on the body of a supposedly bewitched girl, stifling the life out of her.

They are believed as usual, though the people they name are now granted bail rather than sent to prison. But the incident on the bridge has shaken them. These are the last accusations the girls ever make.

On 25 November, the General Court of Massachusetts sets up a Superior Court. But, although Phipps dissolved the Court of Oyer and Terminer, he still makes the same old witch-baiting William Staunton chief judge of the *new* court.

The court is not actually due to sit for another year, but this is an emergency, and Massachusetts passes an act to allow a special sitting beginning on 3 January 1693.

However, there is going to be a crucial difference this time round. Spectral evidence – the evidence of the afflicted girls – is no longer admissible. And, in many of the cases, spectral evidence is the *only* evidence.

Also, for the first time under the new charter, any male householders can serve on a jury, not just church members. There will be a little more scepticism now – a little less Puritan dogma; a little more free thought.

Thirty cases are immediately dismissed for lack of evidence. But people have not stopped believing in witches – far from it. Thirty-six *are* tried, and three people are actually found guilty. Zealous Staunton orders their "speedy execution".

But there will be no execution, speedy or otherwise. Phipps has had enough. He reprieves these three condemned, and five others sentenced earlier by the Court of Oyer and Terminer. When William Staunton hears this, he goes berserk. He storms from the courtroom, shouting, "We were in a way to have cleared the land!"

The trials move to Charlestown, then Boston, and there are no more guilty verdicts.

In May, Governor Phipps orders the release of all those remaining in jail.

However, although many are freed – about a hundred and fifty – many are not. Those who could not pay their jail fees are punished by having to stay in prison. Some have their fees paid by others and are released, but others do not. Some who have escaped the gallows die in prison, condemned by their poverty.

The spell is broken, and the baying mob that crowded into the trials and massed around the gallows becomes again just a collection of ordinary New Englanders. The witch hunt fizzles out. The people of Salem, accused, accusers and afflicted, return to their shattered lives.

Fields and livestock have been left untended and children left without parents, forced to scavenge or rely on the charity of the very neighbours who had joined in the accusations against their mothers and fathers, brothers and sisters.

Many are left ruined after the seizures by the hated Sheriff Corwin and his men, and continue to be treated appallingly. A woman called Ann

Foster, for instance, is reprieved by the judges, but dies in prison. Her son is charged £2 10s to get her body back for the funeral.

Prisoners had to pay for their keep during their stay in the dungeons, the firewood in the hearths, transport to and from the trials and all the costs of the court. Innocence did not free them from any of these debts. For some the experience of prison itself is too much. Little Dorcas Good for one seems never to recover from the trauma of it all.

Chapter 16

Ann Putnam

Now that the witch hunt has ended, does anyone accept responsibility for all the deaths and the ruined lives? Many of the major players do not feel the need to apologise. Sir William Phipps is a politician – he simply blames everybody else. Men like Staunton and Hathorne see nothing to be sorry about.

The jury members who had heard most of the witch trial cases *do* sign an apology. They should have been better informed and directed, they say, by the magistrates and judges not to pay so much heed to spectral evidence. Because of this they have "ignorantly and unwittingly" brought upon themselves and others "the guilt of innocent blood". They say "we would none of us do such things again on such grounds for the whole world."

What about Reverend Samuel Parris? A different man – a man like George Burroughs perhaps – might have been able to dampen the whole witch-hunting frenzy down right at the outset, but Parris was never going to be that man.

Instead of bringing the community together, he helped to create divisions. His sermons pandered to the worst fears of his congregation and he spitefully attacked those who only days before had been respected church members. He seemed to revel in the grisly limelight of the witch hunt right until the bitter end.

In October 1692, the month when the witch hunt effectively comes to an end, Reverend Parris climbs up into his pulpit, just as he had done the previous March. But things are very different now. Now he hopes that "we may on all hands forgive each other heartily, sincerely, and thoroughly, as we do hope and pray that God, for Christ's sake, would forgive each of ourselves."

But it is all too late for Parris. Those who had previously simply disliked him now hate him. Two years later, Parris admits that he had given too much credence to spectral evidence during the witch hunt. He says that he might have spoken "unadvisedly". It is too little, much too late. In 1696 his wife dies, and the following year he leaves the village, taking Betty with him.

On January 14, 1697, there is one of those purging days of fasting and prayer the Puritans are so fond of. Samuel Sewall, one of the trial judges, delivers a paper to the General Court, accepting some of the "blame and shame" for the "tragedy" of 1692. But Sewall knew George Burroughs and should have known he was no more a wizard than he was.

And what about the Putnams? Their names – and the names of their relatives and friends – appear all over the witch hunt and their signatures are on many of the complaints. Did they do this cold-bloodedly, for their own political ends; or were they just so convinced they were on God's side that anyone who opposed them in any way must be on the side of the devil? Whichever, the witch hunt certainly seemed to target many of their enemies.

But one man is particularly responsible; a man who helped create the climate of fear that had incited the hunt in the first place, and helped fan the flames once it started: Cotton Mather.

In 1697, a merchant from Boston called Robert Calef publishes – without the author's permission – Cotton Mather's *More Wonders of the Invisible World*, but adds his own highly sceptical account of the events of 1692, as well as correspondence he has had with Mather.

Calef knows what he is talking about. Like Brattle, he attended examinations and trials and had been at Gallows Hill when Cotton Mather rallied the crowd after George Burroughs's faultless recitation of the Lord's Prayer.

Robert Calef is a modern, rational man; the sort of man that will become much more common in the next century, but one that is still rare in this one. He makes no bones about what he thinks of the afflicted girls. They are a "parcel of possessed, distracted, or lying wenches, accusing their innocent neighbours, pretending they see their spectres."

It is damning stuff. "We have seen a bigoted zeal, stirring up a blind and most bloody rage, not against enemies or irreligious or profligate persons, but against as virtuous and religious as any in this country..." He would have made a great defence attorney for the accused. But of course, they were not allowed a defence.

Cotton has Calef arrested for libel, but the case is dropped. Calef's book is published in London – no printer is willing to touch it in New England – and when it does arrive in Massachusetts, Cotton's loyal father, Increase, has it burned.

Cotton Mather is not popular and he knows it. He even complains in his diary of 1724 that people have taken to naming their slaves 'Cotton Mather' just to annoy him.

And what about those "pretended afflicted" as Calef calls them? After all, if the witch hunt began anywhere, it began that cold winter's night, when the girls gathered excitedly round, giggling about their future husbands.

One girl seems to stands out from the rest: twelve-year-old Ann Putnam. It is she who first saw Rebecca Nurse's spectre, she who first saw Elizabeth Proctor's spectre and she who sent the witch-hunters to Martha Cory's door. It is she who saw the spectres of Burroughs's wives.

In 1706, Ann stands before the hushed congregation in the meetinghouse at Salem Village. The new pastor, Reverend Joseph Green, reads out a statement she has written. Ann's parents are both dead. Years of black looks and sharp words from her neighbours have finally pushed her to speaking out about her part in the tragedy of 1692.

Ann Putnam is now 26 years old. Her parents both died within a fortnight of each other, leaving her to look after her nine brothers and sisters. She has never married – and never will.

"I desire to be humbled before God for that humbling providence that befell my father's family in the year about '92," her statement reads. The Reverend Green might be doing the reading, but all eyes are on Ann Putnam. They have waited fourteen years for this.

She says she was still a child then, and was "made an instrument for the accusing of several persons", and that their lives were taken away, and that she now has "good reason to believe they were innocent persons..." But who was she an instrument of? Of the devil? Of her parents? Of the Putnam family? And did she not have "good reason" to believe those persons were innocent at the time?

"And it was a great delusion of Satan that deceived me in that sad time," it continues, "Whereby I justly fear I have been instrumental, with others, though ignorantly and unwittingly, to bring upon myself and this land the guilt of innocent blood."

This is not a confession; it is an apology. Friendless Ann Putnam is saying sorry, but she is also saying it was not her fault. But was she *really* seeing the things she said she saw? Did she really see Rebecca Nurse's spectre? Did she really see the ghosts of George Burroughs's wives? Was she really "tortured most grievously" by the spectre of four-year-old Dorcas Good as she swore she had been? We will never know.

Ann is saying that she was deluded by Satan, rather than tormented by witchcraft, and that probably seems as good an explanation as anything to most of the congregation. Ann is saying that what she did, she did unknowingly, unwittingly. But at Elizabeth Howe's examination, Ann held up her hand to the judge to show a pin sticking out of it. If Ann is now saying that she believes those people to be innocent, and that Elizabeth Howe's spectre did not stick the pin in her hand, then really she is also saying that she stuck that pin in her own hand. Or maybe one of the other afflicted or even one of her parents did it for her. But Ann is not going to tell us.

The memory of the afflicted girls and their fits are still vivid in the minds of everyone who saw and heard them. The screams and taunts still echo round the room. For the families and friends of those Ann helped to hang, the pain must still be raw. Especially for the family and friends of the Towne sisters, Rebecca Nurse and Mary Easty.

"And particularly," continues Ann's speech, "as I was a chief instrument of accusing Goodwife Nurse and her two sisters, I desire to lie in the dust, and to be humbled for it, in that I was a cause, with others, of the sad calamity to them and their families."

The surviving Towne sister, Sarah Cloyce, has died since the trials, so we will never know what she would have made of Ann's speech. Maybe she would have stormed out of the meetinghouse, as she had done during Parris's sermon all those years before.

"Oh you are a grievous liar!" Sarah had shouted at John Indian at her examination. But no one shouts at Ann Putnam. The Reverend Green finishes reading her statement and everyone agrees to welcome her into the fold as a church member. It is time to forgive and forget. Or at least try.

Ann looks up from beneath her white bonnet. If she knows the truth of what happened in 1692, she is keeping it to herself. But, whatever the truth, maybe the spectres of Rebecca Nurse and the others really do torment her now.

Chapter 17

The Crucible

R everend Green does his best to heal some of
the damage done to Salem Village by the
witch hunt. He brings the feuding families
together and makes Ann Putnam a church
member, encouraging her to read her statement
to the congregation.

Over the years, various survivors or family
members of those who were hanged petition the
General Court to have their names cleared and
for financial compensation. In October 1710,
the General Court reverses the convictions, and
money is finally doled out to some of the
families, but with little fairness. Many who
suffered are not compensated at all.

In the early part of the 18th century, Salem
Village expands eastward and separates itself
from Salem Town to become the town of

Danvers. But it is not a Puritan town. The
Puritans have had their day; Massachusetts has
moved on.

It is not until 1952 that the State of
Massachusetts apologises for the injustice of the
Salem trials. Strangely, even as it does so,
America finds itself in the grip of yet another
"witch hunt".

The House Un-American Activities Committee
(HUAC) was originally created to investigate
pro-Nazi organisations during World War II, but
in the new Cold War with Soviet Russia that
followed, it changed tack to hunt for a new
enemy – *Communists*.

In 1947, the HUAC turned their attentions to
Hollywood and the Screen Writers' Guild,
searching for signs of pro-Communist bias in the
movies. Witnesses who refused to co-operate had
their names added to a "blacklist" that prevented
them from being employed at the film studios.
Many writers were forced to leave the country to

work. Just as in Salem, those who accused others were allowed to go free.

Then America saw the rise of another Cotton Mather. In the 1950s a little-known senator from Wisconsin called Joe McCarthy suddenly made a charge that over 200 Communists had infiltrated the government. The fact that he could not name a single person who was actually a member of the Communist Party did not stop him gaining massive support from the American people.

Just as Cotton Mather, John Hathorne, William Staunton and the settlers of Massachusetts lived in fear of Satan; 1950s America lived under the constant threat of nuclear attack by the Soviet Union. In 1692 it was the devil that was everywhere; in 1952 it was Communists, or "Reds".

Senator McCarthy spent two years questioning government employees, trying to discover if they were Communists and whether they would name others who were. The requirements for a prosecution were a little stricter in 1952 than in

1692, and McCarthy failed to make a convincing case against anyone. But that did not stop people being hounded from their jobs.

Television helped to end McCarthy's witch hunt. It showed him up as a bully; so aggressive and vindictive that people turned against him.

In 1952, a playwright called Arthur Miller, who had been investigated by the HUAC, and given a year's suspended sentence and a fine for refusing to co-operate, was quick to see the parallels between the witch-hunting of McCarthyism and the witch hunts of Salem. The result was his famous play, *The Crucible*.

"Both prosecutions alleged membership of a secret, disloyal group," Miller explained in 2000. "Should the accused confess, his honesty could only be proved by naming former confederates." Just as in Salem in 1692, it was not enough to confess; the examiners wanted names.

The Crucible is not historically accurate – it was never intended to be. Miller just wanted audiences to see "the essential nature of one of the strangest and most awful chapters in human history."

On the 300th anniversary of the hangings, in 1992, a moving memorial was erected in the Old Burying Point cemetery in Salem Town – huge, rough blocks of stone, each inscribed with the name of one of those who were executed.

It was only in 2001 that the last remaining victims of the witch hunt were exonerated. It was only in 2001 that the state of Massachusetts finally accepted the truth of what the accused had said over and over again in 1692: that they were all, every one of them, innocent.

Witch hunts can flare up at any time, anywhere. The victims may not be called "witches" any more – the name of the hunted will change with each century and in each society. But that is the most frightening thing about a witch hunt. You can never be sure the next one won't be hunting you.

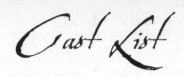

ACCUSED

Bridget Bishop lived in Boston and already had a reputation as a witch.

George Burroughs was born in Suffolk, England and had been the minister in Salem Village where he had fallen out with the powerful Putnam family.

Martha Carrier was from Andover and already had a reputation for witchcraft.

Sarah Cloyce was sister to Rebecca Nurse and Mary Easty.

Giles Cory was 80, the stubborn and bad-tempered husband of Martha Cory.

Martha Cory was 65 and a respected church member.

Mary Easty was sister to Rebecca Nurse and Sarah Cloyce.

Sarah Good had fallen on hard times and forced to beg from her neighbours. She was grumpy and disliked and one of the first to be accused.

Dorcas Good was the four-year-old daughter of Sarah.

Abigail Hobbs was 22 and wild. She was the only one of the accused who seemed to enjoy the limelight.

George Jacobs was in his seventies and was accused by his servant girl and his own granddaughter.

Margaret Jacobs was George Jacobs's 16-year-old granddaughter.

Susannah Martin was from Amesbury and was another of the accused with an existing reputation for witchcraft.

Rebecca Nurse was born in Norfolk, England and was a well-respected church member. She was a frail 71-year-old when accused.

Sarah Osborne was one of the first to be accused.

Elizabeth Proctor was the wife of the successful farmer, John Proctor.

John Proctor was a wealthy farmer, tavern-keeper and trader.

Tituba was Samuel Parris's Caribbean Indian slave and along with Sarah Good and Sarah Osborne was among the first to be accused.

AFFLICTED

Elizabeth Hubbard was the 17-year-old niece of Dr Griggs who first declared the afflicted girls to be "under an evil hand".

John Indian was the husband of Tituba and was likewise a slave in the Parris household.

Mercy Lewis was 17, orphaned by an Indian attack in Maine, and a servant in Ann Putnam's household.

Betty Parris was the 9-year-old daughter of Samuel Parris, the village pastor. She was one of the first afflicted girls.

Ann Putnam Junior was the 12-year-old daughter of local landowner and staunch Puritan, Thomas Putnam. Ann was one of the first to be afflicted.

Ann Putnam Senior was the mother of afflicted girl, Ann, and joined her daughter in accusing Martha Cory and Rebecca Nurse. She was the wife of the influential landowner Thomas Putnam.

Mary Walcott was 17 and daughter of Captain Jonathan Walcott of the local militia.

Mary Warren was servant to the Proctors.

Abigail Williams was Samuel Parris's niece and lived in the parsonage with Betty Parris.

WITCH-HUNTERS

Jonathan Corwin was the magistrate who, along with Hathorne, examined the accused in Salem Village.

Corwin was the nephew of the magistrate and the brutally over-zealous local sheriff.

Thomas Danforth was the 87-year-old deputy-governor of Massachusetts and presided over the examinations of the Proctors and Sarah Cloyce when in Salem Town.

John Hale was the pastor of neighbouring Beverley. He wrote *A Modest Enquiry into the Nature of Witchcraft* in 1702.

Cast List

John Hathorne was a wealthy merchant whose bullying line of questions at the examinations in Salem Village helped produce a rash of confessions and accusations.

Deodat Lawson was Samuel Parris's predecessor as pastor in Salem Village and also published his own account of the proceedings.

Cotton Mather was a famous Boston minister, writer and self-professed expert on witchcraft and demonic possession.

Increase Mather was Cotton's father and like him a famous Boston minister and writer.

Nicholas Noyes was the aggressive pastor of Salem Town. He and John Hale were called in by Parris at the beginning of the witch hunt.

Samuel Parris was Salem Village's first ordained minister, supported by the important Putnam family.

Sir William Phipps was Governor of Massachusetts. He created the Court of Oyer and Terminer.

John Putnam was a captain in the militia, a wealthy landowner and very important in local politics. He was great-uncle to afflicted girl Ann Putnam.

Thomas Putnam was father to Ann Putnam Junior. He was vocal in village politics and a staunch supporter of Samuel Parris.

William Staunton was the leading judge on the Court of Oyer and Terminer. He was a staunch Puritan and determined witch-hunter.

The Witch Hunt Deaths

HANGED

Bridget Bishop
Sarah Good
Martha Cory
Elizabeth Howe
Susannah Martin
Rebecca Nurse
Sarah Wildes
George Burroughs
Martha Carrier
George Jacobs
John Proctor
John Willard
Mary Easty
Alice Parker
Ann Pudeator
Margaret Scott
Wilmot Redd
Samuel Wardwell

PRESSED TO DEATH

Giles Cory

DIED IN PRISON

Sarah Osborne
Roger Toothaker
Ann Foster
Lydia Dustin
(Plus as many as thirteen others)